# the 310:
# BOY TROUBLE

ALSO BY BETH KILLIAN

*The 310: Life as a Poser*
*The 310: Everything She Wants*

# the 310:
# BOY TROUBLE
## beth killian

Pocket Books   MTV BOOKS
New York  London  Toronto  Sydney

POCKET BOOKS, a division of Simon & Schuster, Inc.
1230 Avenue of the Americas, New York, NY 10020

ISBN-13: 978-1-4165-3497-6
ISBN-10:    1-4165-3497-0

This MTV Books/Pocket Books trade paperback edition March 2007

10 9 8 7 6 5 4 3 2 1

Manufactured in the United States of America

For information regarding special discounts for bulk purchases, please contact
Simon & Schuster Special Sales at 1-800-465-6798 or business@simonandschuster.com

For Kresley: good friend and bad influence!

# the 310:
# BOY TROUBLE

# 1

"Well, this trip turned out to be a complete waste of time." Jacinda Crane-Laird flopped back into her seat and waved a crisp hundred-dollar bill at the uniformed flight attendant.

I reached over to grab her wrist. "Will you stop with the cash flash? It's beyond tacky."

"I need a drink," Jacinda huffed. "This is a crisis. Look at me! I have broken my personal rules today, all of them: flying commercial—in *coach* for God's sake;

I'll need to shower for a week to cleanse the filth—to a flyover state so that the Ice Queen here—" she glared at Coelle who, sandwiched into the middle seat between us, stared straight ahead and ignored us—"can snub me. I've earned a kir royale or five, but since they don't make those, I'll settle for a vodka tonic."

"You'll settle for a soda," I corrected.

"*Au contraire.* A stiff drink is in order, missy, and I will not be denied!"

But the flight attendant didn't even bother carding her. "Sorry, miss, but we're preparing for our final descent. I'll need you to put your tray table up and return your seat to an upright and locked position."

Jacinda seethed as the toddler behind us started kicking the seatback.

Next to me, Coelle snickered.

"Yeah, laugh it up, Haughty Von Huffy. Once we get back to Cali, you're dead to me."

"Jacinda," I warned.

"What?"

"We're supposed to be begging forgiveness, remember?" I turned to Coelle and squeezed her shoulder. "We're sorry. Truly, we are."

"Maybe *you* are," Jacinda muttered.

Coelle's dark eyes flashed and her long, straight hair whapped me in the face as she whirled to confront

Jacinda. "I don't care if you're sorry or not. You're moving out of the apartment."

"Hey! Look who's finally talking to me again!" Jacinda peeled the foil off a pack of LifeSavers and popped an orange candy into her mouth. "Communication. Now we're getting somewhere. Don't hold back, babe—I know you're still annoyed about that unfortunate misunderstanding with Quentin—"

Coelle's jaw dropped. "*Misunderstanding*? You traitorous—"

"But that's all in the past now. You've been to the loony bin—"

"It was an eating disorder in-patient facility!" Coelle corrected.

"—and I've done a lot of retail therapy. Plus, I flew all the way out to Okla-frigging-homa to keep you company on your trip back to L.A. I'd say we're even. Can't we just start fresh?" Jacinda offered up her trademark debutante ball smile, all dimples and sparkling green eyes. "Life-Saver?"

After describing in graphic detail exactly where Jacinda could shove her LifeSavers, Coelle turned her attention to me. "Well, Eva? Who's it going to be?"

I buried my face in my magazine. "What do you mean?"

"Who are you going to choose: me or her? Because

you can't be friends with both of us. Not after what happened with Quentin."

I chewed my bottom lip and tried to focus on the paparazzi photo of hottie actor Teague Archer dashing out of a New York nightclub. "Well. Um, listen, we're all upset right now—"

"Oh jeez, here we go." Jacinda crunched down on her candy. "Miss Switzerland."

Coelle raised her chin and addressed me as if she were the queen and I were her scullery maid. "I am willing to forgive you for selling me out to my mother—"

"Thanks," I said dryly. "Considering you were on the brink of physical collapse, that's mighty big of you."

"But I will never forgive *her*." She sniffed in Jacinda's vicinity.

"Forgive me? You should be thanking me!" Jacinda protested. "That guy was a smarmy jackass. I did you a favor."

The plane jolted through a patch of turbulence as Coelle declared, "You have to pick her or me. It's your decision."

I hunched down even farther. "I have to decide right now?"

Coelle nodded. "You have thirty seconds."

"Someone's been reading too many soap opera scripts," Jacinda scoffed, which only fueled Coelle's fury.

"Well, I . . ." I faltered. "Why do I have to choose?"

"I see." Coelle crossed her arms. "You choose Jacinda. Fine."

"What? No!"

"Good choice." Jacinda gave me a perfectly manicured thumbs-up.

I put down the magazine and appealed to Coelle, who was usually the voice of reason. "Come on, don't be like this."

But it was too late. Coelle opened her book (a bulky SAT guide) and refused to look up until the plane landed at LAX, at which point she vaulted over Jacinda and into the aisle, wrestled her massive red carry-on bag out of the overhead compartment (practically knocking Jacinda out cold), and stormed off the plane without a single backward glance.

I exchanged a look with Jacinda across the now-empty seat between us. "'You should be thanking me'? Nice work."

Jacinda dredged through her fringed white leather bag until she found her oversize Chanel sunglasses. "Hey, don't put this all on me. She was gonna be pissed no matter what I said. I told you this trip out to Oklahoma was flushing a perfectly good Saturday down the commode."

"Why couldn't you just apologize? Sincerely?" I

shook my head in disgust. "Now I have to pay the price for your bitchiness."

She zipped up her pink cashmere hoodie and slung her bag over her shoulder as we stepped into the aisle. "Oh, boo hoo. You know I'm the better roommate anyway. More fun, more fashionable . . ."

"More backstabbing, less trustworthy."

"That, too," she agreed cheerfully. "Speaking of which, have you heard anything from Laurel about the *Westchester* job?"

"Not yet." Last week, Jacinda and I had both auditioned for *Westchester County*, a sizzling, scandal-drenched prime-time soap that topped the Nielsen ratings every Thursday night. The show followed a bunch of oversexed trust-fund brats as they navigated the treacherous waters of prep school, prom, and the occasional kidnapping/murder/blackmail scheme.

Although the series usually taped in New York, the producers had decided to film a special spring break episode in L.A., and my aunt, power agent Laurel Cordes, had managed to finagle auditions for Jacinda and me. Jacinda read for the juicy role of the bad girl, and I read for the boring role of the good girl. Just like our real lives. Maybe the casting directors had picked up on my virginity?

"Well, I think I got the part." Jacinda headed for

the nearest coffee stand when we emerged into the airport gate area. "They had me read a few scenes with Teague Archer and I'm telling you, we really had a connection."

"You did?"

"Oh yeah. He kept looking at me with those piercing blue eyes of his, and that accent, my God. He is hott with two Ts."

"Yeah," I agreed glumly as we queued up behind all the other bedraggled travelers at the cash registers. The scent of roasting coffee beans jolted me out of my post-flight torpor.

She slid her sunglasses down the bridge of her nose. "What?"

"Nothing."

"No, I know that look. You're going all angsty. What's wrong? Are you thinking about Danny?"

I coughed. "No."

"Yeah, you were." She rattled off her order for a triple espresso with two shots of chocolate syrup ("I don't ever want to sleep again") and started in on the lecture I'd heard at least once a day since Danny had left me in tears at this very airport. "But you need to knock it off right now. It's time for a major boyfriend upgrade. He was never good enough for you, and he wasn't that cute, either."

She was wrong on both counts, but I knew better than to argue.

"Stop moping around and take a good look around." Jacinda spread her arms to encompass not only the airport, but the entire city. "You have a buffet of available guys at your fingertips. What are you waiting for?"

I mumbled something about grieving time, but she cut me off.

"Your grieving time has officially expired. Now, come on. There's got to be someone you'd consider hooking up with."

There was, actually: Teague Archer. I'd run lines with him at my *Westchester County* audition, too, and I'd thought I'd felt a spark or two. Just like Jacinda. Apparently, he flirted with everything in a skirt. Hmph. I should have known Teague Archer would never go for a girl like me. I tended to attract safe, stable good guys. Like Danny.

And look where that had gotten me.

"Maybe you're right," I said as Jacinda slugged back half the steaming espresso in one gulp.

"I'm sorry." She cupped one hand to her ear. "Could you repeat that? It sounded like you actually admitted I'm right about something."

"I gotta get over Danny. He's not sitting around crying over me."

"That's the spirit!" She raised her fist in victory. "Onward and upward! Let's go back to the apartment, change out of these filthy, coach-infested clothes, and take a nap. The Midwest is exhausting." She wrinkled her pert little nose. "Then we'll go out and find some new prospects. I can get us on the VIP list at Loop."

"Can't." I made a face and waved her cup away as she offered me a sip of her high-octane java. "I'm having dinner with Thomas."

"That's today?"

I nodded. "I'm supposed to be there by five, so I'll have to go straight to Sherman Oaks from here. How much do you think it'll cost to take a cab all the way up there?"

"An airport cab? Ew. Those things are a biohazard and a half. I'll drive you." Jacinda loved any excuse to zoom around town in her sporty little silver Benz convertible.

"Aw. You're so good to me."

She winked. "It's the least I can do, considering you picked me over Coelle."

"I didn't . . . you know what? I'm not having this conversation right now."

"Good. Let's get the hell outta Dodge." Which we did. And while we were barreling up the 405 freeway at heart-stopping rates of speed, the caffeine kicked in and Jacinda got chattier.

"So how's it going with Thomas?" she asked. "Is he everything you thought a long-lost brother would be?"

"Half brother," I corrected. "He got the normal dad. And I don't know yet—I haven't talked to him that much since we first met. He's been studying for midterms, and I've been auditioning, and with everything being so weird with my mom right now—"

"Is she coming to dinner, too?"

"No. God, no. Just me, Thomas, and his dad and stepmom. It's going to be . . ." I searched for a word to describe how I felt about getting to know the sibling I hadn't known I had until I went *Mission: Impossible* on my aunt's file cabinet two months ago. "Fun."

"Say it like you mean it." Jacinda swerved over the double yellow lines into the car pool lane and gunned the motor.

"No, really. I'm excited," I insisted. "I've always hated being an only child and now . . . I don't know. It'll be nice to have someone else besides my mom."

"That's what you say now. But there's a lot to be said for being an only child. I can tell you stories about my sister that will have you sleeping with the lights on."

I frowned. "Hang on, you have a sister? Since when?"

"Since always." Jacinda's customary glossy pout tugged down into a scowl. "Pemberley. She's four years older."

"You're serious?"

"Sadly, yes." Jacinda cut back out of the car pool lane and weaved in and out of traffic like a NASCAR rookie with a death wish.

"Why am I just hearing about this now?"

"Because Little Miss Perfect Pants never makes the gossip columns, unlike certain other members of the Crane-Laird clan. *Pemberley* never does anything risqué. *Pemberley* just sits around in her twin set and pearls all day writing thank-you notes and organizing charity balls for pretentious snobs."

"Not that you're bitter," I said.

"Nooo. And now perfect Pemberley has gotten engaged to the perfect old-money oil scion and she's coming out here to meet his parents."

"Really? Is she going to stay at our apartment?"

"Please." Jacinda snorted. "As if she'd sully herself with the filth of West Hollywood. She'll be bunking in Bel Air with her sorority sister, Muffy."

I laughed. "Shut up. You're lying."

"I wish I were."

"Well, when do we get to meet the Park Avenue Princess?"

Jacinda shrugged and turned up the radio (twangy country ballads; don't ask). "If she ever deigns to acknowledge me in public, I'll let you know."

My cellphone rang before I could ask her what, exactly, she meant by that. "It's Aunt Laurel." I turned the radio off and flipped open my phone. "Hello?"

"Hi, pet!" My aunt sounded breezy and relaxed, no doubt fresh from her latest romp with Gavin, her blond surfer boy toy. "Good news—you got *Westchester County*. So did Jacinda."

I started bouncing up and down in the soft leather seat. "We did?"

"The producers said that Teague Archer loved you. He thought you had real chemistry."

"And by 'you,' you mean Jacinda, right?"

"Nope. You, Evie."

Teague Archer loved me? *Me!* My excitement skyrocketed into elation. Maybe my luck was finally turning around.

"There's only one thing," my aunt cautioned.

Sigh. "Isn't there always?"

"They want you to play the bad girl and Jacinda to play the good girl."

I glanced over at the reckless fashionista flooring the accelerator. "Are you sure about that?"

"Very. And what's more, they want you guys to share a trailer. Guest stars don't get the deluxe accommodations."

"Oh boy."

"I told them you two would have no problem sharing and that you are both going to be delightful to work with . . . *or else.* Oh, and Gavin's scored a speaking part, too. Three clients on one show! They don't call me 'the Tiger Shark' for nothing!"

So she was launching her new boyfriend's acting career single-handedly. I wasn't surprised—Gavin looked like a younger, blonder Nick Lachey. In fact, before I'd caught him half naked and midhickey in my aunt's office, I'd kind of been crushing on him myself.

I tried to block out the image of Gavin in his boxers and Laurel in her black thong and garters (thirty seconds in real time that would necessitate a decade of psychotherapy) and managed a cheery, "Great!"

"Yeah." She cleared her throat. "He's playing your love interest. Well, one of them. Your character really gets around, apparently." Now she was doing the fake cheery voice, too. "You're going to be kissing my boyfriend on TV! Isn't that hilarious?"

"Uh . . ."

"So get ready for your first series job, pet—this should be one hell of an interesting shoot. And listen, you break the news to Jacinda, okay? I'm in no mood for her histrionics right now. I have better things to do."

She had to go smooch Gavin, is what she had to

do. Before I smooched him. In front of a whole bunch of cameras and producers and directors. And Teague Archer. Oh God.

"What's up?" Jacinda demanded when I snapped the phone closed. "Any news on the audition?"

"Not yet," I lied, folding my hands together in my lap. "But hey, no news is good news, right?"

# 2

"Is this it?" Jacinda tapped her fingernails against the steering wheel and let the Mercedes's motor idle in the middle of a quiet, tree-lined suburban street. "'Cause if it is, get out. I can't be seen in the Valley. Some of us have standards to uphold."

"Hang on." I fished a scrap of paper out of my purse and double-checked the address Thomas had dictated over the phone. "Fifty-seven-oh-seven Abbott Circle, white house with blue shutters, second on the right. Yeah, this should be it."

Jacinda tossed back her shiny blonde hair and snickered. "Looks like a soundstage for *The Brady Bunch.*"

She had a point. The rows of orange trees, the perfect green yards, the chalk-scribbled sidewalk, and the abandoned red tricycle on the driveway gave this neighborhood a certain "aw-shucks" wholesomeness.

"Thanks for the ride," I said as I climbed out of the convertible.

All I got in response was the sound of tires squealing against asphalt.

I hurried past the white picket fence (for real), up the tulip-lined walkway to the front door, where I rang the bell and tried to imagine what sort of sitcom cliché might be waiting inside. A Stepford wife with a pink apron and matching heels? Carol Brady herself?

The door swung open and Thomas greeted me in fraying jeans and a Cal State Northridge T-shirt. I hadn't seen him since my mother first dragged him to my doorstep several weeks ago in an attempt to atone for years of absentee parenting by producing the one thing she knew I wanted most in the world: a sibling. But when I looked up at my half brother (I was five nine, so he had to be at least six two; evidently, height ran in the family), I didn't feel an instant spark of kinship. If I'd passed him on the street, I wouldn't have felt any frisson of recognition.

"Hey." He ushered me into a low-ceilinged foyer strewn with bright plastic building blocks. "Come on in."

"Hey," I said back, pausing to inhale a cinnamony, mouth-watering aroma that I hoped would turn out to be pie. Thomas and I looked at each other for a few seconds, then he leaned in for what I thought was going to be a hug, so I leaned in, but then he pulled back, so I did, too, stumbling a bit over a red block.

"You okay?" he asked, not quite meeting my eyes.

I nodded.

"Did you find the place okay?"

"Yeah, your directions were good. Thanks."

We both stared at the floor, fidgeting. You could practically hear the crickets chirping.

"So, um . . ." I groped for a conversation starter. "How were midterms?"

"Okay." He shrugged. "How was your trip to Ohio?"

"Oklahoma," I corrected. "It was okay."

"That's good."

"Yeah."

Why oh why couldn't I have had a sister? What did boys *talk* about, anyway?

"How 'bout those Patriots?" I tried.

He looked startled. "Football season's over."

"Oh. Right."

A petite, square-jawed woman in khakis and a crisp green linen blouse stepped into the foyer. With her pale skin and expensively cut red hair, she looked more like Nicole Kidman than Carol Brady. "You must be Eva. I'm Karen, Tommy's mother. Well, stepmother." She paused. "Marisela's his mother, of course. But I love him like my own."

I tried to pry my hand out of hers, but she had a grip like a bouncer at the *Vanity Fair* post-Oscar party.

"Relax, Mom," Thomas murmured, ducking his head. "And don't call me Tommy."

"I am relaxed," Karen trilled, flashing all her teeth as she smiled at me. "It's such a pleasure to meet you."

"Thanks for inviting me over." I winced as she tightened her handshake of death. "I've been dying to meet you guys."

"You look just like your mother."

"Don't worry, I'm nothing like her," I said. "I promise. For starters, I'm sane."

"Of course you are!" But she finally exhaled and relinquished my poor, mangled hand. "And I'm sure Marisela is a lovely woman."

Ha. I shot a knowing glance over at Thomas, but he didn't smirk back. Oh right. He didn't realize yet that our mom was the emotional equivalent of a five-car pileup on the freeway.

"Dinner's almost ready; why don't you come meet the rest of the family in the den while I finish setting the table?" She shoved Thomas in front of her before leading me down a cheerful yellow hallway covered in family photographs. Weddings, birthdays, graduations . . . all the big milestones were here, captured in high-gloss Technicolor, with everyone beaming and waving to the camera. This was the family I could have had if I'd been born first, instead of Thomas. A sharp splinter of envy wedged into me.

As we approached the den, I heard the bouncy beat of a child's TV program. Karen kept darting furtive glances over her shoulder at me, as if I were about to whip out an ax and hack her to bits.

"Sorry for the mess; there's no such thing as a clean house when you have a preschooler." The sunny family room was cluttered with picture books, stuffed animals, and more plastic blocks. A little girl with curly red pigtails and denim overalls hopped from foot to foot in front of the television, which was broadcasting a cartoon sing-along of "The Wheels on the Bus" at deafening decibels. On the couch sat a balding, stocky man in a white polo shirt and glasses. He looked shy and kind, and as soon as we entered, he got to his feet and offered a handshake.

"Hi." His grip was firm, but not crippling like Karen's. We made eye contact and he smiled, displaying slightly crooked lower teeth. "I'm Graham."

"Thomas's dad," I finished softly. Which made him my . . . nothing, really. We weren't related, even as a stepfamily. He was my half brother's father. Just another in the long list of men my mother had entertained herself with in the late eighties. I tried not to stare, but I couldn't imagine my mother draping herself all over Graham the way I'd seen her do with Tyson, her latest conquest. My mom went for rock stars in leather pants and CEOs in Italian suits. This guy seemed so meek and mild and, well, *normal.*

He took off his glasses and rubbed the lenses with a handkerchief. "This is a little awkward, huh?"

"A lot awkward," I agreed, grateful that someone else finally acknowledged this. "But I'm so glad to meet you guys. I didn't know I had a brother until last month—"

"We didn't know about you, either," Graham said. "All these years, and I had no idea Marisela had another baby."

"She did a good job keeping me a secret," I said. "No one knew. Even her boyfriend thought I was her younger sister."

"And yet, here you are!" Karen crossed her arms tightly.

"Here I am." I knelt down to say hi to the little girl, but she had her eyes squinched shut and was belting out "The Wheels on the Bus" at the top of her lungs.

"That's Maggie," Thomas volunteered. "You'll be seeing her on *American Idol* in ten years."

"Oh, no." Karen shook her head. "No one in this family will be going Hollywood."

"*Mom.*" Thomas looked mortified.

"What?"

"Eva's an actress."

"You are?" Karen took a few steps back.

Graham raised his eyebrows. "You are?"

"Not really," I hedged. "So far, I've only done one commercial. I graduated high school early—long story—and I didn't know what to do while I was waiting to start college, and my aunt runs this talent agency out here . . ."

"Wait a minute." Karen narrowed her eyes. "Was that you in the commercial where the girl's dancing around in her underwear?"

Wince. "Yeah, that's me."

"You did a national commercial? Cool." Thomas seemed impressed. "Have you done anything else?"

"I just found out I got cast for a few episodes of *Westchester County.* They're filming a special spring break sequence out here."

"Can I come visit you on the set?" he asked. "Maybe I'll get to meet Caitlin Hoffman. She's hot."

"Sure," I agreed, so happy to have found a common interest with Thomas that I indulged in some shameless name-dropping. "My roommate's going to be in it, too. You might have heard of her: Jacinda Crane-Laird?"

"Oh my God." Karen's pale face went even paler. "The one who's always in the gossip columns? She's your roommate?"

Too late, I remembered that mentioning Jacinda would not exactly bolster my argument that I was nothing like my mom. "Well, yeah, but I, uh, barely know her. We don't hang out or anything. It's not like I'm out partying with her every night." I crossed my fingers behind my back.

Graham did me the huge favor of changing the subject. "You probably get this all the time, but you look exactly like your mother. Doesn't she, Karen?"

"She does."

"I'm nothing like her," I insisted. "I swear! I know you probably hate her, but—"

"Oh, we don't hate her," Graham said. "We're so thankful she gave us Tom. I mean, yes, it was a surprise when she turned up one day with a baby—"

"No warning, no advance notice, just popped up out of the blue," Karen added shrilly.

"But we'd never change it for the world." Graham seemed so calm and wise and paternal. My envy for Thomas's life doubled.

"Everything turned out for the best," Karen said. "We like our life just the way it is."

"I'm not going to make any trouble for you," I promised. "I'm very responsible. Ask anyone. I was valedictorian of my high school class. Well, before I left, I mean."

Thomas looked like he was saying a silent prayer that the floor would open up and swallow him whole.

"Okay, then." I bolted toward the dining room. "Who needs help setting the table?"

Ninety minutes later, Thomas's parents had stopped treating me like a recently escaped convict, and my vow to lose five pounds before filming started for *Westchester County* on Monday had disintegrated in the wake of Karen's homemade butternut squash ravioli.

"So I had just passed the CPA exam, and one of my buddies from college said he had a job for me." Graham turned to Karen. "Cal Young, remember him?"

Karen rolled her eyes. "The guy with the gold chains and the shiny shirts?"

"Yeah, that's the one." Graham chuckled. "He had just started to manage a bunch of bands. He would troll Sunset every night, looking for the hot new thing."

I sighed. "And he found my mother?"

"No, he found Apollo Grimm." He paused, waiting for Thomas and I to ooh and ahh.

I tried to be polite. "Wow."

"Okay, maybe Apollo Grimm was before your time." Graham folded his napkin and set it neatly beside his plate. "But they were *the* hard-core metal band in the early eighties, and when Cal got them a deal with a big record label, they needed someone to help them manage their money. That's where I came in."

I nodded. "And you went to one of their concerts, right? And my mom was backstage?"

Graham and Karen exchanged a look. "Something like that."

I turned to Thomas. "Marisela goes through rock stars like other women go through lip balms."

Graham flushed. "Well, anyway, there was an after party, and then an after-after party, and Cal kept encouraging me to stay fifteen more minutes and bond with the band so they would trust me with their royalty checks, and—"

Karen scraped back her chair, collected a stack of plates, and stalked into the kitchen, muttering under her breath.

Graham took off his glasses and started wiping the lenses again, even though he'd just cleaned them before dinner. "I apologize, Eva. I don't want you to get caught in the middle of all this. It's just—the whole thing with Mari was . . . she was a little wild, yes, but she was sweet. Very sweet. Please don't think that I . . . that we . . . I called her, after that night. I wanted to see her again." His eyes shone when he talked about her.

No wonder Karen got huffy. Thomas's dad was still a little bit in love with my mom and probably always would be.

*Sucker.*

Thomas summed up the rest of the story in a flat, clipped voice. "And Dad didn't know about me until a year and a half later when Marisela called him from New York and said she was checking into rehab and he had a son and she needed someone to give him a stable home life and, fast forward twenty years, here we all are."

My jaw dropped. "So you knew? All this time, you knew Marisela was your mother?"

Thomas studied his floral patterned placemat. "Yeah. We didn't talk about it much, but yeah. I always called my mom—Karen—'Mom,' though. It wasn't that big a deal."

I tapped the tines of my fork with my fingertip and asked the question that had been eating away at me since I first shook Thomas's hand at my West Holly-wood apartment last month. "Did she ever contact you before? Did you guys—"

"Uh-uh." He shook his head. "Never."

"Mari called me a few weeks ago," Graham said, sounding rather proud of this. "Twenty years of nothing—Karen and I had sent photos and Christmas cards to her through your aunt's agency over the years, but we never got any response—and then, apropos of nothing, she calls, invites me to brunch, tells me she has a daughter, and asks if she can 'borrow' our son for a day." That sappy, wistful look was back. "She really loves you, Eva."

Seriously, what did my mom *do* to these men? Were they brainwashed? Hypnotized? So crazed with hormones that they didn't have a single firing synapse left in their brains?

"Oh yeah," I deadpanned. "It's like one, endless season of *Gilmore Girls* at our house." I focused on Thomas, who didn't seem at all curious or resentful about his biological mother. "Wasn't it hard, never hearing from her? Didn't you always wonder who and what and where she was?"

"I dunno. Not really." He shrugged. "I mean, I'd see photos of her occasionally; it wasn't a deep dark secret, but . . ." He lifted one shoulder. "I have a family."

He appeared to be telling the truth. He hadn't spent every night of his childhood lying in bed, making up elaborate, Disney-flavored fantasies about winning the county spelling bee or starring in the second grade play and finally catching the attention of a mother who couldn't be bothered to venture east of L.A. or west of Manhattan because "Mommy's got to work Fashion Week, darling." Maybe guys were just different that way. Maybe they didn't crave maternal approval.

Maybe you didn't need the fantasy if you had the real thing.

The conversation kind of dried up after that. Karen never reemerged from the kitchen and Graham suggested that we skip dessert "till next time." Yeah. Like I was ever going to see the inside of that house again. When Thomas drove me back to West Hollywood (talk about awkward—our entire dialogue consisted of me saying "thanks" and him saying "no problem"), I was relieved to find the apartment empty. No Coelle, no Jacinda, no drama. Just the promise of a hot bubble bath, a pair of ibuprofen to tame the tension headache that had kicked in right about the time Karen had started slamming plates around, and . . . the big envelope with my name on it resting on the kitchen table.

I opened the flap to find a *Westchester County* script titled "Spring Break." There were two notes scribbled on the first page—one in my aunt Laurel's neat, tight handwriting ("Have your lines memorized by Monday or heads will roll. Which reminds me, you need to get your highlights touched up ASAP.") The other note was a loose, slanted scrawl: "Looking forward to our scene on page 27. I'll bring the breath mints. Break a leg, T."

"T?" T as in Teague? I flipped to page 27, and sure enough, the script called for a scorching make-out session between street-wise Hollywood vixen Bella Santorini and Jake, the character Teague had made famous with his slow, wicked smile and piercing blue eyes.

My heart ping-ponged around my chest as I reread the stage directions: BELLA PULLS JAKE TOWARD HER AND KISSES HIM PASSIONATELY. SHE YANKS OFF HIS SHIRT, THEN HER OWN, AND THEY SUCCUMB TO TEMPTATION.

I was going to seduce *Teague Freaking Archer.* Me! And he was supplying the breath mints! Sure, I'd have to strip down to my bra in front of an entire camera crew, but this was network television, right? How much skin could they really show? This was going to change my life! This was going to make up for everything that had ever gone wrong.

Then I saw Aunt Laurel's second note, the one she'd scribbled on a pink Post-it and stuck inside the script: "You're filming on location at UCLA. Have fun with the rush-hour traffic."

UCLA. Home of Danny Bristow and the fragmented remains of my broken heart. Future home of my steamy love scene with the guy that reduced everyone—even Jacinda—to a swoony, babbling puddle of lust. Maybe

I'd run into Danny during a scene break. I'd be freshly made-up and coiffed by the show's glam squad and he'd be skulking around, scrawny and unshaven, too miserable to eat or shave or even play baseball once he realized that dumping me had been the biggest mistake of his life.

His jaw would drop at the sight of me and he'd beg me to take him back and—oh, what the hell—he'd break down and sob that if only he had the chance to meet me at the Somerset Hotel again, things would be different this time, so different!

But I'd be like, "Sorry, dah-ling, I can't talk right now— I've lost my voice from screaming with passion in the arms of my new man. You've met Teague Archer, right?"

And then Danny would spend the rest of his life comparing all his future girlfriends to me and none of them would ever measure up.

Hooray for Hollywood.

# 3

Rumor has it that teen heartthrob Quentin Palmer has moved on from brainy beauty Coelle Banerjee. Quentin stepped out in style at Frost nightclub on Friday with not one but <u>two</u> buxom blondes. His stick-thin ex-squeeze has been keeping a low profile while she preps for pilot season auditions. Can she make it to prime time?

"Hey, did you see this?" I spooned up a bite of organic oat bran flakes (we were out of Lucky Charms so I'd had to raid Coelle's cabinet) and waved the Sunday edition of *South of Sunset,* West Hollywood's lowbrow, must-read tabloid, at Jacinda as she trudged down the tan carpeted stairs of our tiny, clothes-strewn apartment. "Look who made the G-Spot."

"Don't try to distract me with that trashy rag!" Whoa. Two minutes out of bed and already she was waving her fists in fury. I'd never seen anyone look so threatening in black lacy underpants, a pink tank top, and bare feet. Her ponytail was messy, her face was smudged with last night's eyeshadow, but her green eyes were sharp and alert. "What the hell is the meaning off this?" She shoved a copy of the *Westchester County* script into my face.

I choked on my cereal. "Oh, yeah. That. Well, I was going to tell you yesterday afternoon, but—"

*"You're* playing Bella and I'm playing *Lucy?"*

"Lucy's a great role." I tried to soothe her. "You have more lines than I do—I counted. So really, you're—"

She read aloud the script's character descriptions. "'Lucy Hanson, seventeen: A sweet, innocent daddy's girl who has been sheltered from the seedier side of life in L.A. Bella Santorini, eighteen: a vampy sex kitten who always gets her man and lets nothing get in the way of a good time.' This is just wrong! They must have gotten our head shots mixed up!" She rolled up the script and brandished it like a steak knife. "*I* am the sex kitten around here! *I* always get my man! And you . . . well, talk about sheltered and socially inept . . ."

My sympathy went straight out the window. "There's no mistake, Jacinda. They want me for Bella. Me. Laurel told me herself."

"Ha! Wait until they see your pathetic attempts at flirting! You couldn't hang on to a man with both hands and a vat of superglue."

"Teague Archer begs to differ," I said sweetly.

She slammed the script on the coffee table, spilling half a mug of hot coffee. "*Westchester County* is bullshit! The writing sucks and the editing is atrocious. No one even watches it anymore. Wait. I take that back. You know who watches it? Twelve-year-olds with enlarged pores and no social skills who sit home on Thursday nights, sanitizing their retainers and journaling about how they can't wait to finally get their period."

"You watch it," I pointed out. "Every week."

"That was before they cast me as an insipid little priss," she snarled. "I hate that stupid show."

"You're seriously complaining about landing a guest role on a major network show? Are you PMSing or what?

It's good money and good exposure for your career." I crossed my arms over my comfy, oversize Leighton College T-shirt. "Besides, the script even says Bella is brunette and Lucy is blonde." I looked pointedly from my black ponytail to her platinum one.

That's when she broke out the big guns. "Bissy Billington was right about you," she hissed. "You're nothing but a backstabbing part-stealer!"

She might as well have pitched a grenade across the sofa cushion. Bissy Billington, former Little Miss Sweet Sixteen from the great state of Texas, was a lovely little dimpled blonde with a penchant for all-white outfits and a vicious streak a mile wide. Ever since I'd inadvertently beaten her out for a commercial (one hundred percent *not* my fault) my first week in Hollywood, Bissy and her Cruella De Vil stage mother had made it their lives' mission to, and I quote, "destroy" me. (Yes, this business tends to attract the drama queens.)

I glared at Jacinda. "As of this moment, you officially have *two* roommates not speaking to you."

While I was trying to decide whether I should dump my cereal milk on her head and make a run for it—I'd learned the hard way that Jacinda's wispy blonde exterior belied a sinewy brawler who didn't pull her punches—the doorbell chimed.

I flounced over to the kitchen sink and deposited my bowl, expecting Jacinda to answer the door. But she threw herself down onto the sagging lavender sofa, grabbed the remote control, and clicked on the television.

"Someone's at the door," I said.

"I thought you weren't speaking to me. Come on, don't be a quitter."

I stalked across the apartment, flung open the front door, and found myself face-to-face with a sleek, willowy blonde so preppy she probably had a Ralph Lauren logo permanently imprinted on her butt. She wore an expertly cut blue shirtdress accessorized with a simple strand of pearls and a blue headband.

"Hello, I'm Pemberley Crane-Laird." She held out one lily-white hand. "Such a pleasure to meet you."

While I shook her right hand, I ogled the massive diamond adorning her left. I couldn't *not* notice it—that thing could sink the *Queen Mary.* "I'm Eva Cordes." Jacinda remained rooted to the couch. She seemed transfixed by the TV screen, oblivious to her own flesh and blood standing there on our doorstep. I cleared my throat. "So you're Jacinda's sister. I've been dying to meet you."

"Don't believe anything that little minx tells you." Pemberley's tinkly laugh sounded forced. " 'Our little scandal puss,' that's what Daddy calls her."

"How adorable." I tinkly laughed right back, then stepped back to let Pemberley inside. "Jacinda, look who it is!"

Jacinda's lips had thinned to a narrow white slit.

"Sorry about the mess." I kicked aside some of Jacinda's thousand-dollar castoffs. "There's three girls in this tiny apartment and—"

"Oh, heavens, don't apologize." Pemberley waved me off with a little flick of her wrist. "You *are* sweet. But I know how Jacinda goes through clothes—just like she goes through boys. There's no keeping up with her! It's like our mother always says—"

Jacinda jumped in before I could find out what, exactly, their mother always said. "Would you shut up already? There's no one from the society page here to report your lame little bon mots."

Pemberley straightened her headband and kept right on smiling. "I'm so glad to see you, Cinda." She opened her arms for a hug.

Jacinda didn't get up.

"Ooh, you haven't seen my ring yet!" Pemberley wiggled her left hand. "Isn't it to die for? It was Chip's great-great-grandmother's. A family heirloom!"

Jacinda turned back to the TV.

The mounting tension was killing me, so I tried to supply the responses my roommate couldn't be bothered to give. "Wow, that is gorgeous. When did you get engaged?"

Pemberley's eyes lit up. "Valentine's Day! His name's Chip Pettigrew, and his family lives in Montecito, up by Santa Barbara. Well, actually, they have several homes—one in Montecito, one in Laguna Beach, and a winery up in Napa that—"

"We get it, we get it," Jacinda snapped. "You bagged yourself a rich one. Well, enjoy the money, because with that guy's gene pool, your kids are gonna look like inbred llamas."

"*Jacinda.*" Pemberley's pink cheeks turned crimson. "We are in public. Try to control yourself for once."

Jacinda made a big show of thumping her bare feet down on the coffee table. "Look around, fool. We're not in public. We're in my apartment. I can do and say whatever I want."

Pemberley threw a mortified glance in my direction.

"Eva already knows I'm a snarky, déclassé slag," Jacinda assured her. "In fact, she's not even speaking to me at the moment. So unclench, princess."

Pemberley started twisting her pearls. "Don't you dare speak to me that way!"

"I'll speak to you any way I want. You're so superficial and saccharine I could throw up."

"I come all the way out here to see my only sister

and this is how you treat me? My God, Jacinda, look at you! Living in squalor, showing up topless all over the Internet . . ."

"Just because I don't have a Phi Beta Kappa key up my ass—"

Pemberley grimaced. "Stop. You're nothing but a vulgar, vapid Barbie doll with a credit card where your soul should be."

"Oh, yeah? Well . . . well, you've gained weight! Your arms look like thighs!"

I slunk out the front door, closing it softly behind me, and left the dueling blonde tornados to shriek it out.

Coelle was walking across the cobblestone courtyard outside the apartment. When we made eye contact, she tilted her chin and pretended not to see me.

"Hey." I raised one hand in greeting.

She marched past, wearing a sweaty T-shirt, yoga pants, sneakers, and her iPod. She must be coming back from a run. Or therapy. Or her volunteer work at the Humane Society. I wouldn't know.

"What've you been up to?" I ventured.

"Hmph" was her only reply.

"Oh come on. Don't be mad. Please? I didn't *do* anything!"

She powered toward the apartment without a backward glance, her glossy black hair gleaming in the bright morning sun. When she stepped over the threshold, I heard pottery shattering and high-pitched screeching like chimpanzees on amphetamines.

Coelle backed out of the apartment, wide-eyed and pale, and yanked the door closed behind her.

"See?" I said. "I tried to warn you."

She shot me a filthy look, then double-timed it out of the courtyard and back to the sidewalk.

"Bye!" I called after her. "Nice talking to you!"

Okay. So the current tally of people with whom I was not on speaking terms now included: Coelle, Jacinda, my mom, my dad's whole family, Danny, Bissy Billington, and . . . uh . . . probably Thomas's stepmom. Socially, I wasn't doing much better in L.A. than I had in Massachusetts.

I climbed into my ride, a gigantic white, serial killer-esque van (mockingly dubbed "the Goose" by Jacinda in happier times), and headed for the hills—as in Beverly—to see the one person who always had plenty to say to me.

# 4

"Hi, pet." Aunt Laurel met me in the high-ceilinged, marble-floored entry hall of her palatial, Mediterranean-style house. "How was the trip to Oklahoma? How was dinner with Thomas's family? Did you get the script I messengered over?"

"It was, uh . . . we, uh . . ." I tried to stop staring, but I couldn't wrest my gaze away from her turquoise silk robe, bare feet, and tousled hair. I'd never seen the woman out of a suit. I honestly thought she slept in black Armani blazers. "What are you wearing?"

She tightened the belt of the clingy robe. "Oh, well, it's Sunday, you know, so . . ."

Then I noticed her fingernails, which were lacquered bright red. "Since when do you wear nail polish? I thought you said bright colors were a sign of weakness?"

"Only in the boardroom," she amended. "But it's the weekend, right?"

I stared at Laurel for a few long moments, wondering why I had never noticed before how much she looked like my mom. They had grown up together in small-town Massachusetts but had turned out so differently—my mom a boozy, debt-ridden ex-model and my aunt a rich, ruthless power agent who fed on gourmet sushi and her underlings' fear—that you would never suspect they were related. But now that Laurel's thick, wavy brown hair was loose instead of twisted up in a chignon and her eyes had lost their Machiavellian glint, I realized that she shared my mother's high cheekbones and arched eyebrows. She wasn't quite as thin as my mom, but then, who was? At five foot nine with a body that could squeeze into sample sizes when I needed it to, I was considered the short, dumpy member of the Cordes clan.

I checked my watch. "You just got out of bed?"

She nodded, beaming.

"You didn't wake up at the crack of dawn to go over contracts or suffer through some grueling personal training session?"

"Nope."

"Okay." I looked around for Gavin. "Where is he?" Before she could protest, I added, "Don't play innocent with me. I've only see you looking like this once before, and that was in your office when—"

She threw up a hand. "We do not speak of that day. Agreed?"

"Agreed. So where is he? And I don't mean Rhett." Right on cue, Laurel's yappy, snappy black teacup poodle raced in from the kitchen and attacked my sneaker as if it were a big Kobe steak topped with bacon.

"Yow!" I shuffled backward, but the little beast sank his teeth into my sock and hung on. "Has he had his rabies shots?"

"He's not rabid, he's just a little overexcited." Laurel scooped up the poodle and cradled him like she would a baby. "He loves you! You wuv Evie, don't you, my widdle punkin?"

Rhett looked at me and raised one lip in a silent snarl. Thank God he was only eight pounds or he would've ripped out my jugular long ago.

I got back to the topic at hand. "So where's Gavin? I know he's in here somewhere, 'cause—"

"Hey." Gavin, who had clearly overheard the entire conversation, stepped out of Laurel's study. He wore faded jeans and nothing else. "How's it going?" His beautiful blue eyes glazed over with concentration as he tried to remember my name. "It's Eva, right?"

"Right." I leaned back against the doorway and tried to focus on the massive crystal chandelier, the hideous mural of Tuscan peasants picking grapes . . . anything but Gavin's tanned, muscle-bound chest. Between the floppy blond hair, the perfect manly profile, and the bulging biceps, he looked like, well, like a lot of other devastatingly handsome aspiring actors in Hollywood. But he also had a certain something—I didn't know if it was charisma or confidence or what—that had caught my eye (and Laurel's) the very first time I met him.

"How's it goin'?" He shoved his hands in his pockets, all casual. "I haven't seen you since—"

"We do not speak of that day," my aunt repeated. "Let's all get dressed and have lunch."

Gavin jerked his head toward the study. "I'll just grab my T-shirt and I'm good to go."

Laurel started up the stairs. "Why don't you two catch up while I get ready? Now that you're both cast in *Westchester County,* you have plenty to talk about. Just do me a favor and refrain from rehearsing the big kiss until I get back."

I looked at Gavin.

Gavin looked at me.

"This is going to be weird, isn't it?" I nibbled my bottom lip.

"Yeah." He crossed his perfect arms over his perfect chest. "Laurel's great, but she's definitely the jealous type. Has she had really bad breakups or something?"

"Probably." I sighed. "That seems to run in the family."

I spent Sunday night trying to memorize my lines (which felt sort of like cramming for a final exam for a first-period class I'd slept through all semester) and reported to the set of *Westchester County* early Monday morning, armed with my dark sunglasses (*tres* Hollywood) and a year's supply of mouthwash and gum. Since I didn't know when the director planned to film the make-out scenes with Gavin and Teague Archer, I intended to stay minty fresh at all times. I might not be a boy magnet like Jacinda, but no one could accuse me of being a bad kisser. In fact, if Danny's response in the past had been any indication, I was an excellent kisser. The two of us used to kiss for hours; long, slow, deep kisses while our hormones raged and our hands roamed—

*Stop. Stop right there.*

I was about to guest star on the coolest show on TV, in which I would be smooching two guys hot enough to scorch your retinas, and I refused to ruin the experience by obsessing on the one guy I couldn't have.

It was hard not to think about him, though, considering we were filming on his home turf. Danny was finishing his sophomore year at UCLA, and as I walked past the coffeehouse and the bookstore, I couldn't help scanning the groups of students milling around the open, grassy walkway. Every time I saw a tall guy in a dark blue baseball cap, my heart sped up.

"Stop," I warned myself out loud. I didn't miss him. I never loved him. Yeah. Keep telling yourself that.

When I turned the corner, I spotted the makeshift set—a cluster of cameras, lights, and low-slung trailers. The beefy, black-shirted security guards waved me through when I flashed my set pass, then directed me to check in with a wiry guy in cargo pants, a white T-shirt, and a few days' growth of facial hair who was barking orders into a walkie-talkie.

"Hi," I said when he paused to breathe. "I'm Eva Cordes."

"Eva Cordes . . ." he scanned the call sheet on his clipboard. "You're playing Bella Santorini?" He scribbled something next to my name, then scratched his chin. "I'm Rich, the first assistant director. You'll come see me first thing every day when you show up for work. I'm the gatekeeper."

I smiled. "The gatekeeper for what?"

He looked deadly serious. "For everything. Listen, we're waiting on another girl from your agency." He squinted down at his clipboard. "Jacinda Crane-Laird. You have any idea where she is?"

I hadn't seen Jacinda since yesterday afternoon. "I thought she was here already."

"Nope. Her call time was an hour ago." Rich gnawed on the end of his pen. "I thought the Allora Agency was supposed to be this paragon of talent and professionalism?"

"It is," I assured him, hitching up my jeans. "Definitely. *I'm* on time, see?"

He muttered something about flaky actors under his breath, then sent me on to Damien, a tall, painfully thin man with red hair and an all-black outfit. I had to watch my step to avoid tripping over the cables and wires snaking across the lawn.

Damien turned out to be the show's dialogue coach. "How many years of training have you had and with whom?" was his first question.

"Uh . . ." To date, I'd had approximately two weeks' worth of acting and movement classes with a tattooed, purple-haired lunatic before I'd been forced to drop out due to unwanted sexual advances from a scrawny, street slang-slinging Bel Air homey who fancied himself the next Eminem. "I'm still kind of new to this."

Surprisingly, this seemed to please him. "Then you have no objection to employing the Method while you're here?"

"Of course not."

When he smiled, his face, teeth, and lips all blurred into one pasty white blob.

"Excellent. We won't be filming your first scene until this afternoon, but you should spend the morning rehearsing and meeting the rest of the cast." He pointed a long, spindly finger toward a huge, white trailer in the nearby parking lot. "Teague is expecting you."

I looked down at my jeans, sweatshirt, and flip-flops in dismay. "Right now?"

"Right now. And we do not keep Teague Archer waiting."

I slicked on some lip gloss and pinched my cheeks as I made my way toward Teague's trailer, which was at least as big as our West Hollywood apartment. When I climbed the flimsy metal steps and rapped on the door, I could hear the frenetic brass beat of jazz music blaring from within.

The music stopped and the door swung inward.

"Hi," I started, my voice shaking just a teeny bit. "Um, sorry to interrupt, but Damien said I should—"

Without a word, Teague reached out, pulled me into the trailer, dipped me down like we were championship salsa dancers, and kissed me right on the lips.

# 5

The kiss was quick—no tongue, no groping—but overwhelming. Jacinda and Coelle had warned me that most actors who seemed sexy in the movies were insipid tools in real life, but when Teague Archer kissed me, I felt something I'd never felt before. It was like, all of a sudden, the rules I'd followed my whole life no longer applied. *Anything* could happen.

Luckily, he had a firm grip on me or I would have toppled over from the shock. I knew I should be outraged, but when he set me back on my feet and gave me that raffish grin, all I could think of to say was, "Oh my God."

"Oh my God is right." He winked. "Glad we got that out of the way."

I kept staring at him, my eyes so wide they felt like they were about to pop out of their sockets and roll away.

"Page twenty-seven," he offered by way of explanation. "Now we don't have to be weird about it."

I could detect a hint of an accent, but not the full-on Aussie drawl he played up during his TV interviews. With his dark blue jeans and faded gray T-shirt, Teague dressed like any other twenty-one-year-old in SoCal. His face, however, set him apart. Even Gavin seemed blah by comparison. And it wasn't just the thick black hair, startling blue eyes, and perfect body (I could see the faint outline of his pecs and biceps through the cotton shirt-he was *that* cut). Teague radiated a deep, raw confidence that made me feel like right here, right now was the most exciting place in the world. Aunt Laurel would probably call it stage presence. Me? I preferred to think of it as sweltering hotness.

But I had dabbled with swelteringly hot guys before, and all it had gotten me was social infamy and a one-way ticket from Massachusetts to Los Angeles. So I cleared my throat and took a small step back toward the trailer's door.

Teague laughed at my apprehension. "No worries; what we just had was the no-bullshit introduction. Here's the way I see it: If you had come in and shook my hand and we had talked about the weather and run lines for an hour, we'd be wasting our time. Instead of listening to each other, we'd be thinking about the inevitable kiss, wondering what it'd be like. But this way? We get all that out of the way up front, and now we can have a proper chat." He flopped down onto one of the black leather sofas angled around a book-laden coffee table and nodded to the chair next to him. "Make yourself comfortable."

I perched on the very edge of the cushion and watched for any more sudden moves. My lips felt all tingly, like I'd been to the dentist and the novocaine was starting to wear off.

Teague stretched his arms out along the back of the sofa. "So how *is* the weather out there? Still sunny and seventy-five?"

I crossed my legs and stacked my hands on my knee. "Listen, I appreciate you putting in a good word for me with the casting people, I really do, but I don't kiss guys I just met thirty seconds ago."

"Of course you don't." He leaned over to the mini-fridge next to the sofa and extracted two sodas, one of which he offered to me. "But your character does."

I grabbed the icy cold can with just my thumb and index finger, careful not to touch his hand. "Yeah, well, I'm not my character."

The devilish grin was back. "Don't let Damien hear you say that. As far as he's concerned, we *are* the star-crossed, wayward teens of Westchester County."

Oh boy. "Is that what he meant by Method acting?"

Teague raised an eyebrow. "What's this? Damien let you escape without a five-hour tutorial on Stella Adler and Uta Hagen?"

I blinked. "Who?"

He laughed. "Mate, you are in for a world of hurt. Here." He rummaged through the books heaped on the coffee table and pressed one into my hands.

I read the title. *"The Stanislavski System."*

"Your new bible. Learn it, live it, and prepare to spend the next two weeks as Bella Santorini, Hollywood temptress. On-set, off-set, during your lunch break . . . you've got to start thinking like a heartbreaking, back-stabbing hellcat."

I *knew* Jacinda should have gotten this part. "But I can't!"

"Sure you can." There it was again: that calm, convincing confidence.

"Trust me, I don't know the first thing about break-ing hearts. I'm boring and polite and hopelessly good."

He shook his head. "If you were hopelessly good, you wouldn't be able to play a character like Bella so well. I saw you at that audition. Beneath that sweet, innocent exterior lurks the soul of a bad girl."

I rolled my eyes. "Do you hit on everyone you meet?"

"I'm not hitting on you; I'm telling the God's honest truth."

"I'll take that as a yes."

"We have chemistry," he declared. "And that's a good thing, considering you're supposed to seduce me."

"On the show," I reminded him.

"And then you're going to drop me flat and run off with another bloke and leave me a broken shell of a man." He snatched up his soda and slugged it back in feigned despair.

I smiled. "Well, sorry in advance about that. But that's what we bad girls do."

"Exactly. It'll be fun. And no offense, but you look like you could use a little fun."

"Yeah." I sighed. "I probably could."

He leaned forward. "Let me guess—there's a story behind that sigh. Starring you, your good girl ways, and some shiftless whacker who wasn't good enough for you anyway."

I thought about the fiasco I'd caused last month with Danny and my friend Jeff. "Not exactly. Let's just run lines, okay?"

"Oh, come on. You can tell me."

My cheeks burned under the intensity of his gaze. "I just met you."

"Yeah, but we've already kissed."

"Because you ambushed me." Even to my own ears, I sounded prim, like my grandmother when she used to lecture me about how nice girls didn't show their midriff in public. That's all I'd ever be—a *nice girl*. Ugh. "Look, I'm sorry to be so, you know, boring, but I'm just a little freaked-out right now. This is my first day on a TV set, I've never met a movie star—let alone kissed one—I don't know jack about Method acting, the assistant director's in a snit because my roommate's late, and yes, if you must know, I just crashed and burned a relationship with this guy who really . . ." I stopped and fanned my face with my hand as I started tearing up ". . . he wasn't too good for me. At all."

Teague had stopped smiling. "Hey. Okay. We'll just—"

My cellphone rang and cut him off. Caller ID flashed "Mom." Just what I didn't need.

I ignored the ring tone and stared up at the trailer's ridged metal ceiling for a full minute, waiting for Teague to mock me or call security and demand I stay at least fifty feet away from him for the rest of the shoot. But when I finally risked a look in his direction, he was rooting around in the sofa's many throw pillows.

"What're you doing?" I asked.

"Oh, I went to this awards show last night, and they gave out a whole mess of swag to the presenters, and . . ." He shoved his hand down between the cushions and emerged with a sleek, square silver contraption. "Here we go."

"What is that?"

"Everything, basically: phone, text messenger, e-mail, MP3 player, even stores photos and up to ninety minutes of digital video. It's new. They're calling it the Filament. Enjoy."

"Oh, I couldn't possibly—"

"You can and you will." He pressed the gadget into my palm, his skin warm against the inside of my wrist. "I'm going to do piss-all with it. Do you know how many new phones I've gotten for free this year?"

I shook my head.

"I lost track after number ten. So take it—a girl like you shouldn't have to haul around a mobile from the days when dinosaurs ruled the earth. No wonder you're crying." He dived back into the cushions. "Hang on—I've got a gift certificate for a year's worth of service in here, too. Found it." He slapped two pieces of paper down next to the phone. "Sweet as a biscuit. Here's your activation code and look at this-a voucher for dinner for two at Dice."

"Isn't that the club they're always writing about in *South of Sunset?* I haven't been there yet."

He feigned horror. "What? You've lived in L.A. how long?"

"A few months."

"And you haven't been to Dice yet? Why would you deprive yourself like that?"

I brushed the hair out of my face. "Well, I've been busy with work and family stuff and that guy I don't want to talk about."

"The guy who never took you to Dice, you mean? What kind of sorry excuse for a man is that?" He jumped to his feet and held out a hand to me. "That's it—we're going. You, me, Friday night."

Holy crap. Teague Archer just asked me out. It was official: up was now down and black was now white.

"You can't say no," he warned me. "You don't have a choice. We're going."

Part of me was ready to put my hand in his and run off to Dice right now, but another part of me—the part that remembered what had just happened with Coelle and Quentin—resisted.

He must have picked up on my conflicting emotions, because he leaned back against the wall and looked me right in the eye. "Eva, whoever that other guy was, forget him. I'm going to show you the fun side of Hollywood. No strings, no angst. Just what you need. You're . . . how old are you?"

"Eighteen," I supplied. "Not old enough to get into Dice, probably."

"Don't worry about that. Don't worry, period. You're eighteen and you're going to have the time of your life." He offered his hand again and this time I grabbed it without hesitation.

Our little interlude came screeching to a halt as a voice outside yelled, "I *am not* late! And even if I am, it's only because that stupid parking lot attendant made me leave my car eighty thousand miles away and hike across the entire campus! In stilettos! So if you're going to give me a lecture, you better give me a physical therapist to go along with it!"

A low, soothing male voice tried to reason with Jacinda, but she was having none of it.

"Eva!" she cried. "Hey! Cordes, where are you?"

Someone started pounding on the trailer's thin metal door, the thumps reverberating through the room like a kettle drum.

"I know you're in there, missy! I know what you're

doing! Step away from my future boyfriend and no one gets hurt!"

Teague cocked his head as if he were a safari guide listening to an oncoming stampede of elephants. "What the bloody hell is that?"

I sighed. "That would be your other new co-star. Allow me to introduce my roommate and best frenemy, the Notorious J.C.L."

6

Two seconds later, the door slammed open and Jacinda charged in with her fists clenched and her eyes blazing. Clearly, the security team had underestimated her. Two dazed-looking bodyguards blinked up from the bottom of the steps.

"Aha!" She jabbed her freshly manicured finger toward my face, practically gouging out my eye. "I show up ten minutes late and you're already throwing yourself at the star."

I bristled. "Okay, first of all, you're more like an hour late, and second of all—"

"Second of all, she's not throwing herself at me." Teague stepped in between us, shielding me from Jacinda's razor-sharp French tips. "I'm throwing myself at *her*, actually."

"Teague!" Jacinda flipped her blonde hair and instantly downshifted from tempest to temptress. "Hi! Delightful to see you again."

While I was peering over Teague's shoulder, I couldn't help noticing that he smelled freakishly good—like he'd managed to bottle the fresh, crisp wind blowing in from the ocean. He smelled like sailing and sunscreen.

Jacinda flashed her dimples and batted her eyelashes (unlike me, she'd obviously put in several hours' worth of primping before showing up on set. Her flirty green sundress and strappy gold sandals put my threadbare jeans and ponytail to shame.) "You know we have lots of friends in common in L.A.—Tessa Kilgore, Jared Duzak, Nanette Demarchet . . ."

The hit parade of name-dropping just went on and on. No wonder I hadn't seen the girl in twenty-four hours—she must have been chained to her computer, cyberstalking Teague. As I watched her working her smile, working her body, working her social connections, I realized that this was why she always got the guy. It wasn't just charm and good looks; Jacinda honed the craft of man-wrangling the way I used to labor over my AP calculus homework. Once she was finished with Teague, he wouldn't even remember my name.

I exhaled softly, put on my gracious loser face, and had started to make my exit when Teague reached back and squeezed my hand.

Jacinda's eyebrows snapped together.

"Good to see you again," Teague told her. "You're Eva's roommate, right?"

"Eva is *my* roommate," she corrected. "I'm the fun one. And since we're going to be working together, I thought we should get to know each other bettter."

She whipped out a tube of shiny red lip gloss and pouted like a cover model while she slooowly applied a fresh coat.

Teague turned to me. "She's the fun one?"

I scowled. "Well, yeah, technically, I guess she is, but—"

He nodded. "That explains it."

"What?" Jacinda and I said together.

"Everything." He grinned.

"Eva's a sweetie, but she was miscast," Jacinda stage-whispered, as if I couldn't hear every syllable. "If you like bad girls, look no further." She winked and leaned over to give him a better view of her cleavage. I glanced at the couch cushions, hoping Teague had stashed a bunch of throwing stars and nunchakus in there along with all the free cellphones, because I was about to go ninja on Jacinda's ass.

Before Teague could respond to the shameless boob flash, the assistant director poked his head in the door. "Everything okay in here?"

"Fine, mate."

"Well, they need you in hair and makeup in five minutes, so . . ." As the two guys stepped outside to discuss scheduling specifics, I confronted Jacinda.

"What do you think you're doing?" I hissed. "Ambushing the star? Beating up bodyguards? You're going to get fired!"

"Ha! Getting fired is for plebs. They're lucky to have me and they know it!" She planted her spike heels in the beige carpet and put one hand on her hip. "Stay away from Teague. He's mine."

"Oh really? I saw him first."

Her smile went from predatory to pitying. "You saw him first? That's the best you can do?"

"Okay, I *kissed* him first. How about that?"

She gasped. "You did not!"

"Did, too." I smirked.

"Did not!"

"Did, too."

"Well, it doesn't matter *what* you did, because I am going to—"

"Wait." I cocked my head and listened. "Shut up a minute." The hustle and bustle outside the trailer had stopped. An eerie silence had fallen over the set, which could only mean one thing: the entire crew was eavesdropping and my aunt would be getting word that her clients had started a catfight in Teague Archer's trailer within thirty minutes of arriving on their first day. I'd have no choice but to join the witness protection program.

"This is not cool; we have to get out there and behave like adults." As I strode out the door, Jacinda stuck out one of her tiny, couture-clad feet and tripped me. I tumbled down the three steps and sprawled facedown in the damp, muddy grass while she stepped over me, her nose in the air.

But her little victory strut came to an abrupt halt when Teague rushed to my side and helped me to my feet.

"Thanks." I brushed off my hands and knees. "Sorry about . . . well, everything, really. We were just leaving."

"You two are rougher than a rugby scrum." He looked impressed. "I guess it's true, what they say about Allora Agency girls."

"What do they say?"

He laughed. "I'll tell you later, maybe Friday night."

Jacinda whirled around, her face ashen. "You two are going somewhere Friday night?"

"Right now, we're just going to the makeup trailer." Teague led me past the lighting crew, all of whom were pretending to be working while they stared at the Allora girl smackdown. "See you in a few."

I allowed myself to be tugged along, sparing a quick wave back at my roommate, whose expression flickered between fury and disbelief.

"But . . . but I'm the fun one!" she choked out. "I'm the bad girl!"

"Bad girls are a dime a dozen." Teague slid his hand across the small of my back to my hip. "What I want is a challenge."

Five hours later, I was back at my car and halfway in love. Or at least, serious like. *Something.* After an entire day of "filming"—which actually consisted of a rehearsal and a lot of standing around while the director worked out blocking and lighting and camera angles—all I could think about was Teague Archer. His eyes, his hands, his kiss . . . that boy was trouble. Not to mention a total player. He was the polar opposite of my type.

And yet.

Maybe I really did have a bad girl trapped inside, clamoring for her chance to escape.

"Look out, world." I laughed to myself and threw an extra swagger into my step. "It's a whole new Eva."

And then I froze, midswagger, as I saw the vintage gold Mercedes-Benz. Boxy and ancient, with rust creeping in at the wheel wells and a dent on the passenger-side door.

I'd recognize that car anywhere. How many half-restored, door-dented 1984 Mercedes could there be on this campus? My car keys dug into the soft flesh of my palm as I scanned the parking garage for Danny.

But all I saw was a trio of college girls with matching blonde highlights and blue sorority sweatshirts. He wasn't here. False alarm.

So why did I feel like I was about to hyperventilate and keel over right here on the oil-stained concrete?

*Forget him. It's a brand-new Eva.* I managed to unlock the Goose and buckle myself into the driver's seat with shaking hands. UCLA was a huge school. The odds of running into him here were infinitesimal. No need to panic. Save that for Friday evening, aka date night with Teague, who would probably kiss me again. And who knew what else we'd do . . .

My cell rang, startling me, and I answered it without checking caller ID. Big mistake.

"Evie!" My mother's voice was refined but lilting, kind of a cross between Marilyn Monroe and Princess Diana. "Hi, sweetie! How was your first day on set?"

When I paused, she charged ahead with, "How's everything going with Thomas? I heard you had dinner with his family. How was it?"

"Other than the fact that they kept looking at me like I was the devil incarnate, not bad."

"See? I knew you all would get along. Graham's such a great guy."

I cleared my throat. "Yeah, it was a regular barrel of laughs."

"Hey, did you get to meet his new wife?"

"I'm not sure I'd really call her 'new,' but—"

"What was she like?" Mom paused. "Was she prettier than me?"

I gritted my teeth. "No one's prettier than you. As you're well aware."

"Well, we can't all be *Vogue* material, right?" No wonder Mom didn't have any girlfriends. "So was she sweet? Stodgy? Totally generic? Come on, spill."

I turned the keys in the ignition and backed the Goose slowly out of the parking space. "Is there a point to this conversation?"

"Don't be difficult, darling, I'm asking a perfectly civilized question."

"No, you're not! You just want me to rip on Thomas's stepmom and reassure you that Graham never got over you and you're the fairest of them all, like the wicked queen in *Snow White*."

She perked right up. "You think he never got over me?"

"Why do you even care? Are you that insecure?"

"Don't you talk to me that way!"

I threw the van into drive and headed for the parking garage exit. "Why not?"

"Because . . . because I'm your mother, that's why."

"Really. Name one maternal thing you did after they cut my umbilical cord."

She exhaled impatiently. "Evie, I'm not going to have this tired old argument again. Ugh. I cannot wait until you're out of this sulky, self-righteous adolescent stage."

"Ditto." I turned out onto Sunset Boulevard and headed toward West Hollywood.

"Listen. Baby girl." Her voice got all syrupy again, and I knew what that meant: she wanted something. "Let's not fight."

"Too late," I reminded her. "We've been in a fight since last month. I'm still mad about what happened at the car wash, don't think I'm not."

"You're always mad at me," she said. "Sooner or later, you're going to have to get over it, because all this rage is very unhealthy. You're going to give yourself a heart attack. Or brain cancer. Or a stroke. Or . . ."

"Yeah, yeah, yeah." The Goose rolled to a stop as traffic backed up at a red light. "Just tell me what you want and let's get this over with."

She pouted. "I don't want anything, Evie. God. I just enjoy chatting with my darling daughter."

"Mom." I rested my forehead on the steering wheel and massaged my temples. "I know you didn't call just to chat. So tell me what you want. Daylight's burning and we both have places to go and people to see."

She sniffed, all wounded and put-upon. "I want to have dinner with you and Thomas. Together. Is that so evil? Is that so selfish?"

"Depends on your motivation."

"We need a little family time, baby. Just the three of us. So we can, you know, bond."

My Marisela Cordes manipulation detector went on red alert. Whenever she started talking about bonding and family harmony, she was gearing up for something truly outrageous.

"You'll have to talk to Thomas about that," I hedged. "He might be kind of annoyed that you abandoned him all those years ago and now you just want to waltz back into his life and pretend like nothing ever happened. He might still be holding a grudge, you know?"

She laughed dryly. "No, he's not, that's you."

"Well, I can't speak for him, okay? I have no idea if he'll want to do dinner or not."

"Don't worry, he'll do it."

"How can you be so sure?"

"Because he's male."

She had a point. No mere man could say no to my mom. Boyfriends, bosses, her father, her son . . . they were all putty in her hands. Thomas would always forgive her, no matter what she did because—I could hear it now—"She means well, Eva, and everyone makes mistakes . . ."

"We don't have to do this, Mom," I pleaded. "We don't have to pretend we're normal. Just be honest with me, and I'll—"

"Oh, stop being such a buzzkill and have dinner with me." She giggled. "I have a surprise for you."

"Oh no."

"You're going to die, absolutely die!"

"Oh *no.*"

"But you have to have dinner with me to find out what it is."

I gripped the steering wheel so hard, my knuckles went white. "I don't want to know what it is."

"Yes, you do. Trust me."

"You make me insane," I strangled out.

"Is that a yes?"

# 7

"It's official," I announced as I trudged through our apartment's front door. "I'm an idiot."

Coelle didn't look up from the paperback she was reading on the couch. Clad in a tight, low-cut black minidress, accessorized with dramatic kohl eyeliner, drippy diamond earrings and Tolstoy (I caught a glimpse of the front cover: *War and Peace,*) she looked like a cross between Nicole Richie and Morticia Addams.

"Coelle?" I tried again. "Hello? I'm here, I'm admitting I'm an idiot."

She didn't glance up from her book. "Mmm. I couldn't agree more."

"Well, are you going to start speaking to me again?"

"I didn't hear any apology."

"Oh my God. You're going to make me beg?"

She continued to ignore me.

Screw this. I hadn't done anything wrong and I wasn't going to degrade myself. I had pride. I had principles.

Two minutes later, I cracked open a diet soda and collapsed on the sofa, practically in Coelle's lap. "Okay, I'll beg, I'm sorry, all right? I'm not even sure what I'm sorry for, since Jacinda is the one who—"

"You're sorry for siding with her against me," Coelle supplied.

"But I didn't side with her! You're the one who said I had to choose!"

She lifted one expertly shaped black eyebrow. "For someone who's supposed to be apologizing, you don't sound very sorry."

"Ooh . . . you . . . this . . . *fine*. Fine! I was wrong, you were right, a thousand pardons. Happy now?"

She finally met my eyes. "Aren't you supposed to be an actress? That was the fakest remorse I've ever seen."

"Yeah, well, I guess I'll have to wait a few years for

that Golden Globe. Which reminds me: Do you have any books on Method acting?"

"Tons." She closed her book, leaving her index finger between the pages to mark her place. "Why?"

"It turns out *Westchester County* has an acting coach and he's like the second coming of Stanislavski. Not that I even know who that is, but Teague said—"

"You saw Teague Archer today?" Coelle was usually a jaded little cynic, but even she seemed a bit fluttery when it came to my new castmate.

"I not only met him, I kissed him. Actually, he kissed me. And he asked me out for Friday night. Like a date! And look." I dug the shiny silver Filament out of my bag. "He gave me this because he said—"

"Whoa, whoa, whoa." She held up a hand. "Eva Cordes, did you learn nothing from the fiasco with me and Quentin? Thou shalt not date thy costars. That's rule number one, chiseled in stone right next to 'never start a war with the press' and 'always use the back door at the plastic surgeon's.'"

I hung my head. "I know, but . . ."

"But what?"

"But he's Teague freaking Archer!"

"So what? He gives you one swag bag freebie and you swoon?"

I frowned. "How did you know it was a swag bag freebie?"

"I grew up in this industry, remember? I know all the tricks." She patted my hand like I was a wide-eyed toddler. "You can't allow those little trinkets to turn your head. And what are you doing letting him kiss you, anyway? Isn't he kind of rough around the edges for you? I could see Jacinda getting involved with a guy like that, but you . . . ?"

I sucked in a slow, measured breath. "Yeah. About that."

She leaned forward, letting Tolstoy tumble to the floor. "What? What'd she do?"

"Well, she assumed that Teague would want to get with her, since, you know, everyone else does. But when he said that he'd rather go out with me—"

Coelle snickered. "I wish I could've seen her face. Karma is a bitch, baby!"

"So is Jacinda. I'm afraid for my life."

"He snubbed her. I love it!" Coelle rubbed her hands together in glee. "You know what? I changed my mind. Do whatever you want with him. He sounds like a great guy! But don't put out just because he threw a little swag your way. At least wait until he wines and dines you."

I blinked. "I just met him."

She clapped me on the back. "Congratulations, I think you're finally going to lose your virginity."

"Coelle!"

"Just remember to use protection. You have no idea where he's been. Although, if the rumors in *Us Weekly* are any indication—"

"This is ridiculous. I'm not going to have sex with Teague Archer!"

"Why not?"

"Because . . ." Because I was going to have sex with Danny. He was supposed to be my first. Although frankly, the fact that we had broken up was kind of putting a crimp in that plan.

Coelle grinned. "I'm waiting."

"I'm not talking about this anymore," I sputtered. "Let's talk about you. Why are you dressed like a funeral director turned stripper?"

"Callback audition. For a big-budget summer movie. I'm supposed to be the devil."

"Wow. I didn't know Laurel was sending you out for films. And the devil, no less. That's a big deal."

"It would be, if I cared." She stretched out her legs and crossed her ankles over the coffee table. "But I don't. I was a snotty little brat to the casting agent, and I gave the worst reading of all time."

I shot her a look. "If you don't want to be in show

business anymore, why don't you just talk to your mom?"

"Please. You've met my mom. There's no talking to her. She keeps saying college can wait, my real life can wait. The only way she's ever going to back off is if I stop getting work."

"So you're just going to sabotage all your auditions?"

Coelle nodded. "I figure I'll last about two months without a paycheck before Laurel drops me."

"Laurel wouldn't just drop you like that."

"She wouldn't drop *you*, because you're her niece. The rest of us, though . . . if we're not earning, we're wasting her time." She folded her hands behind her head and wiggled her toes. "Good-bye Hollywood, hello college." She nodded down at the massive paperback on the floor. "I enrolled in some extension classes at UCLA. I'm taking world literature and intro to psychology. Next term, I'll take biology, but that has a lab, so—"

"Wow. You're not playing around."

She set her jaw and narrowed her eyes. "I'm *going* to college. With or without my mom's permission. A few more disgraceful auditions like the one I blew today, and I'm home free."

"But you can't leave!" I protested. "If you move out, God only knows who'll move into your bedroom. What if, oh crap, what if *Bissy* moves in here?"

"Relax; Bissy would never go anywhere without her sainted mommy. You should stop worrying about me and start worrying about what's going on with you and your new *lovah*."

"He's not my 'lovah' and I don't know what's going on. And you know what? I don't want to know what's going on." As the words came out of my mouth, I realized that they were true. "I'm tired of stressing and being the responsible one and never hurting anyone's feelings."

"My sister in rebellion." Coelle nodded. "What brought this on?"

I picked at the lint on my sweatshirt. "Nothing, really."

"This is about Danny, isn't it?"

"What? No!"

"Liar. I just spent four weeks in a psychiatric treatment center, and you're more messed up than I am. You've got to let him go, Eva. It's over."

"I know that!"

"Then why do you still get that misty, faraway look in your eyes when I say his name?"

I drew my knees up to my chin. "I don't."

"You do, too." She leaned toward me. "Danny Bristow, Danny Bristow, Danny—"

*"Aigh!"* I clamped my hands over my ears. "Shut up!"

"See?" she crowed. "You should see your face. You look like someone just steamrolled over your puppy."

A sharp knock at the door interrupted out caterwauling. "Pardon me, is this a bad time?"

I peered over toward the screen door, where I could discern the whippet-thin silhouette of Pemberley Crane-Laird. "Hi. We were just, uh . . ." I nudged Coelle and muttered, "Help me out here," but she kept staring at the doorway with her mouth open so wide, I could count her molars.

"Holy crap. You must be Jacinda's sister."

Pemberley folded her hands primly. Today she wore slim black pants with a tailored blue shirt, tasteful pearl earrings, and a small, patent leather handbag that probably cost more than my (so-called) car. She looked like the world's classiest parole officer. "I'm Pemberley, yes . . . delighted to meet you. I left my sunglasses here yesterday, and I hoped to pick them up before Jacinda appropriated them as her own. I've lost more accessories to that little larcenist . . ."

Coelle kept right on gawking. "You look just like her."

"Oh heavens, don't say that. You'll give me a complex." Pemberley forced a laugh as I opened the door. "We're both blonde—*I'm* natural, by the way, *hers* is from a bottle—but that's where the similarity ends. You'll never catch me stumbling past the paparazzi at three A.M. in nothing but a see-through minidress and a tattoo."

"Jacinda doesn't have a tattoo." I felt an odd urge to defend her, even though we were sworn enemies at the moment.

Coelle coughed. "Yes, she does. You just have to know where to look."

"Are you sure?" I asked. "Because I've seen pretty much everything there is to see."

"Who hasn't?" Pemberley shuddered and made a face. "My poor parents. I honestly thought they were going to have to move to Europe after those trashy photos hit the Internet last year. My mother was simply beside herself. It's a miracle any man from a decent family would deign to marry a Crane-Laird after that." She turned her head to wave over her shoulder at a sleek red Ferrari idling at the curb across the courtyard. The driver responded by leaning on the horn, causing a passing jogger to stumble in surprise.

"Sorry, lambikins, I won't be a moment!" she cried, then turned back to us with a look of impatience. "That's Chip."

I eyed the uber-coiffed Man Tan lounging behind the wheel. "Nice guy."

"He is, actually, but he hates to be kept waiting, so I'll just find my glasses and be on my way."

"Don't you want to wait until Jacinda gets home?" I checked my watch. "They were filming the last scene of the day when I left the set; she should be home any minute."

Pemberley shook her head. "It's easier when we don't have to interact, especially with Chip here. I don't think his family would appreciate the social implications."

"You're engaged to the man and you haven't introduced him to your sister?" Coelle pressed.

Pemberley sashayed across the carpet and plucked a pair of black sunglasses from a pile of fashion magazines on the kitchen table. "Oh, here they are. Safe and sound."

We all jumped a little as Chip blasted the horn again.

"Mission accomplished, girls; I should run!" Pemberley air kissed in the general direction of our heads as she ran for the door. "You seem lovely—I'm so sorry you have to live with my sister."

And then she was gone. A few seconds later, we heard a car door slam and the motor rev into overdrive.

"Jeez" was Coelle's only comment.

"I know. She makes my mother look warm and nurturing," I said.

Both of us were silent for a moment. Newfound sympathy for Jacinda trickled into my heart as I considered what it must be like to grow up with a family that was so ashamed of you that they openly apologized to your roommates for your very existence.

"Well, I don't care," Coelle said, crossing her arms. "I'm still mad at her."

"Come on," I wheedled. "Wouldn't you be kind of a hag if you had to live with a sister like that?"

"There's no excuse for what Jacinda did to me." Coelle stood firm. "I will say, though, that if Pemberley's a natural blonde, I'm P. Diddy."

I laughed. "So where is this legendary tattoo, anyway?"

"Let's just say that only Jacinda and her bikini waxer know for sure."

I cringed as Coelle's cellphone rang. "There's a visual I don't need."

"I tried to warn you."

"Do I even want to know what the tattoo's of?"

"Nope. Save yourself the nightmares." Coelle answered her phone. Her expression went from sardonic to stormy to downright scary. "You're kidding . . . no *way* . . . well, call them back and tell them—okay . . . okay, okay, whatever you say."

"What's wrong?" I asked when she clicked off the line.

"I can't believe this!" She threw up her hands. "What

on earth is wrong with people? How can anyone possibly be that stupid?"

"Uh-oh. Was that your mom?"

"It was your aunt. They just called and offered me the part!"

I glanced at her revealing minidress. "For the devil?"

"Yes."

"Which goes against your new subversive master plan?"

"Yes! I can't believe this. I freaking carpet bombed that audition and they *hire me?* Those twisted, sadistic . . ." She grabbed a throw pillow and throttled it with both hands. "I'm in hell! I'm in hell!"

"Close." I rubbed her back consolingly. "You're in Hollywood."

# 8

The next morning, I got my booty to the *Westchester County* set bright and early, the better to get my hair and makeup started before Teague arrived. Fake eyelashes and the right shade of lipstick were a girl's best friend, that was my motto. Especially if said girl was competing with a gorgeous, surgically enhanced celebutante for a guy who probably had bruises on his ankles from all the fans throwing themselves at his feet.

I grabbed a Styrofoam cup of coffee from the craft

service table and breathed in the sharp scent of fresh Colombian roast as the hairstylist went to work with her flat iron. Five minutes later, Thomas called. Maybe he'd seen right through my mother's ruse. Maybe he was calling to plan a show of solidarity against maternal manipulation.

"Hello?" I answered, crossing my fingers.

"Hey, Eva." He sounded tense, and I could hear honks and revving motors in the background. He must be driving to class on the freeway.

I waited for him to initiate some friendly small talk, but after several seconds of silence, I realized he was waiting for me to do the same. "Hey, so, um, thanks for dinner the other night. Thank Karen, I mean."

"No problem."

Another long pause. God, this was excruciating.

"So what's up?" I tried.

"Nothing. You?"

I was guessing that all the drama with Jacinda, Coelle, Pemberley, and Teague Archer would not impress him. "Not much."

"Oh."

"I'm, uh, glad you called."

"Yeah. Your mom asked me to."

I yelped as the hair stylist singed the tip of my ear with the flat iron. "Stop fidgeting," she commanded.

"She wants to have dinner," Thomas continued. "The three of us together. Like family night or something."

"Yeah, about that . . . let me save you a little time and a whole lot of therapy: there is no 'family time' with her. There is only 'Marisela time.'"

He didn't say anything. All I could hear was the freeway.

"Hello?" I prompted.

"I'm here," he said. "But I don't want to get into the whole thing between you and Marisela."

"You don't want to . . ." My jaw dropped open. "What did she say to you?"

"Nothing." He sounded defensive. Clearly my mom had already converted him to the dark side. "But it's just dinner, right? It could be cool. We'll catch up and she says she has lots of pictures and stories and stuff . . ."

"So trusting," I murmured. "So naïve."

"What's that?"

*Grr.* "I said, when and where are we meeting?"

"Friday night at Regency. Like seven o'clock?"

"Ooh, Friday's not gonna work. I have a thing. A date."

More freeway noise.

"Thomas?" I yelled into the receiver.

"Yeah, it's okay. I understand." But he was obviously disappointed. "We'll do it some other time. Whenever."

"I'm really sorry," I said, meaning every word. "Honestly, if it were any other day . . ."

"It's cool." He sounded crushed. "Your mom said you'd make excuses."

"I'm not making excuses! I really have a—"

"It's okay. I get it."

"No, you don't!" I forced myself to pause and silently count to five. "What about Saturday?" I tried. "Sunday?"

"I'll be in San Diego this weekend. My band's playing."

I tilted my head, earning another sizzling burn from the flat iron and a withering look from the stylist. "You're in a band? Why didn't you tell me that before?"

"I don't know. It's kind of weird to just bring it up. Even though we're related, we're not . . ."

"Yeah." I sighed. "I know."

Ten more seconds of freeway noise and the guilt got to me. "Okay. I'm in. Let's do dinner on Friday."

"No, just forget it."

"No, I want to. Family comes first, right? I can reschedule my date."

"You sure?"

"Of course." I hoped. I prayed.

"Okay, great. See you Friday." He seemed excited when he said good-bye, and I reminded myself that this was the reason I had come to L.A. To find my family. To get answers about my past. Not to hooch around with cute boys of questionable moral integrity.

Speaking of whom . . .

"Look what the cat dragged in." Teague, looking heartbreakingly handsome in his black rugby shirt and scruffy morning stubble, sat down in the chair next to me and helped himself to a sip of my coffee. "The bad girl in training."

"Hi." I nibbled my lower lip. "About Friday night . . ."

"You're dropping me already? But I haven't even had a chance to screw up yet. Come on, give a bloke a fair go."

"Family thing," I said weakly.

"On a Friday night?"

"My family's kind of unusual. It's a long story."

"Playing hard to get?"

Rather than explaining, I decided to try out a few of the Method acting tips I'd read last night. What would Bella Santorini do? I looked up at him through the sheaves of hair that the stylist had pushed over my face. "I don't play hard to get—I *am* hard to get."

"Then I'll have to weasel my way into your good graces." He took my hand and stroked the inside of my wrist with his thumb. "What might that take, do you think?" He was barely touching me, but somehow it felt more intimate than when he had kissed me.

*Breathe. Remember to breathe.* "Give my coffee back, for starters."

He burst out laughing, and I joined in, and he was still holding my hand and murmuring into my ear when a no-nonsense voice interrupted our idyllic little moment.

"Eva Dominique Cordes, what is going on?"

It was Aunt Laurel, and she was pissed. The red nail polish and carefree demeanor from the weekend were long gone. Today she was all business in pointy-toed pumps, a black power suit, and a dour expression.

"What?" I yanked my hand away from Teague's. "I didn't do anything."

I braced myself for a lecture on the perils of dating my costars—after which I would have to shrivel up and die of humiliation—but she didn't even acknowledge Teague. "According to the assistant director, you did plenty. He told me all about your brawl with Jacinda on-set yesterday."

"Oh. That."

"Yes, that." She folded her arms and drummed her fingers on the sleeve of her blazer. "*That* is going to ruin my agency's reputation. *That* is wasting my time, which I have to spend coming all the way to Westwood this morning to yell at you instead of signing contracts and negotiating multimillion-dollar deals. *That* is completely unacceptable."

"Okay, I know, but I swear I didn't start—"

She threw up a hand. "Don't you dare say it's not your fault."

"But it's not!"

My aunt smiled grimly at the hairstylist. "I'm so sorry to interrupt, but could I possibly steal this one away for just a moment?"

The hairstylist ran for cover as Laurel strode around the chair to face me and proceeded to go Defcon One. "It's never your fault, Eva, have you noticed that trend? It's always Jacinda, or your mother, or your grandparents. You're always the helpless victim."

"But I—"

"You said you wanted to be an actor, and that means you show up, you do your job, and you keep your personal life off-set. You're my niece and I love you, but I will not have you acting like a spoiled legacy brat. You want respect? You want a good reputation in the industry? You have to earn it."

Teague leaned into my personal space and flashed his magazine-cover grin at Laurel. "She earned my respect. And so far, I'd say her reputation is stellar."

My aunt plastered on her highest-wattage networking smile. "Teague Archer! What an honor to meet you!"

She grabbed his hand and shook so hard, he winced a little. "I'm a big fan."

"This is my aunt," I told him. "Laurel Cordes."

"The Allora Agency, right?" He stretched out his long, denim-clad legs and tipped back his chair. "You guys are repping some exciting projects over there."

"Absolutely!" Laurel purred, handing over her business card. "We're very exclusive, but we always have room for the best and the brightest. Let's have lunch while you're in town."

She and Teague went into full schmooze mode, each exclaiming over the other's unique brilliance. I rolled my eyes and sipped my coffee.

Before Laurel could finish fawning over Teague and get back to ripping me up one side and down the other, Gavin wandered up behind me. In his baggy cargo shorts and rumpled white T-shirt, he looked like he'd just rolled out of bed. Which he probably had—Laurel's bed. I wondered what they talked about when they weren't, you know, naked. Did she mesmerize him with facts and figures about the weekend box office receipts? Did his tales of surfing and waiting tables make her go weak in the knees? They seemed really into each other. But how serious could they be if they were keeping their whole relationship secret?

"Hey," Gavin said, sounding tired and a little hungover. "How's it goin'?"

"Treachery, catfights, wrongful accusations," I said. "Same old, same old."

"Cool."

"What about you?"

He pushed his floppy blond bangs out of his eyes. "I'm filming my first scene after lunch today. I'm super-psyched."

We both knew our kissing scene was scheduled to film in a few days but neither of us mentioned it.

"You'll do great," I assured him.

"Yes, he will." My aunt swooped back into the conversation. She introduced Gavin to Teague, then returned her focus to me as her smile sharpened. "Now, gentlemen, if you'll excuse us for a moment—"

"Laurel, there's no need to give Eva hell for what happened yesterday." Teague was addressing my aunt as a peer, as if *he* were my agent. "You know how these on-set rumors get blown out of proportion. It was nothing."

Laurel set her jaw. "That's not what I heard."

"Don't worry about it. I'll keep her in line." He threw me a sly smile. "And just look at her—no wonder other actresses get jealous."

"Yeah," Gavin agreed. "She can't help that she's young and beautiful."

My aunt froze. *"What?"*

Gavin yawned. "If she were old and wrinkly, no one would be starting with her, that's all I'm saying."

Laurel grabbed Gavin's forearm and physically dragged him away.

"She's just too young and ravishing? That's her problem?" My aunt's voice was high and clipped. "And what exactly does that make me?"

"Hey, calm down," Gavin soothed. "We're not talking about you."

"Oh right. Because I fall into the 'old and wrinkly' category, is that it?" Laurel rummaged through her purse, presumably for a set of brass knuckles, before whirling around and stalking toward the assistant director.

"Babe! Wait! What'd I do?" Gavin followed her and put a hand on her shoulder. They started glaring at each other and gesturing wildly.

"Is something going on between those two?" Teague asked.

"Sort of." I sighed. "It's complicated."

"Care to elaborate?"

"Not really. The Cordes women have a very sketchy track record when it comes to dating. I am starting to think it's genetic."

"I'll consider myself warned."

* * *

The good news was, I got to leave the set a lot earlier than anticipated that afternoon, along with half the cast. The bad news was, the reason for our early departure was Jacinda's repeated need for retakes. She either couldn't or wouldn't deliver her lines on cue.

"Cut!" the director barked after another flubbed scene. "Cut, cut, cut. We're breaking for fifteen minutes, everyone. Damien, teach this girl her lines or find me a replacement by Monday."

While Damien murmured that everything would be under control by tomorrow, Jacinda went on the offensive.

"It's her fault," she announced, pointing at Caitlin Hoffman, the show's female star. "She messed up her dialogue."

Caitlin glared right back at my roommate. "I didn't mess up anything. It's called ad-libbing."

"It's called making crap up because you forgot what you were supposed to say." Jacinda's face was splotched with red and even after an hour and a half in the makeup chair, her forehead was beaded with sweat like she'd just finished a 5K sprint. She also looked jarringly sweet and modest—wardrobe had outfitted her in a knee-length pink plaid skirt, a pink crew-neck sweater, and ballet flats. Between the outfit and the preppy ponytail in her hair, she could have been Pemberley's twin.

But I knew that mentioning Pemberley would only make matters worse. I sidled up to Jacinda and asked, "Do you want me to help you with your lines?"

She shot me a look that could have microwaved me from the inside out. "Don't start with me, Cordes. A, you're dead to me. B, I'm not the one who needs help with my lines." She jabbed her index finger at Caitlin Hoffman. "*She's* the one who needs help."

Caitlin turned to Rich, the assistant director, with her palms turned out. "Did you hear that? I can't work with prima donnas."

"*Knock it off,*" I hissed to Jacinda. "They're going to fire you."

"Since when do you care?" She swished her ponytail right in my face, giving me a mouthful of hair. "You'd love it if I got fired. Then you could have you-know-who all to yourself."

"I'm right here, you know." Teague waved from the sidelines. "I can hear you."

"Jacinda." I grabbed her wrist and dug my fingernails in as Damien approached, looking surly. "Stop this right now. You have to calm—"

"Don't touch me!" She narrowed her green eyes to thin little slits. "You are not the boss of me. You're an insignificant little wannabe with semidecent bone structure and a big-shot aunt." She lifted her chin. "*I am Jacinda Crane-Laird: model, actress, It girl. I don't take orders, I give them.*"

The director, who had been walking away from us, stopped in his tracks.

Desperate to defuse the impending crisis, I clapped my hand over Jacinda's mouth. She chomped down on my fingers like Rhett the poodle.

"*Ow!*" I yelped. "What the hell—"

"I don't need your help," she informed Damien. "I can act circles around everyone else on this pathetic excuse for a show, especially Caitlin Hoffman."

Audible gasps all around.

"That's it." The director rolled up his sleeves. "You're fired."

"You can't fire me, I quit!" Jacinda threw her script on the grass and ground the heel of her prissy ballet flat into the pages. "If you're going to fire someone, I suggest you start with Caitlin, followed by your hackneyed team of writers because the roaches in the catering truck could come up with better material than this!"

The director turned to me. "Is she on narcotics? Is that what this is about? Because if our insurers find out—"

"No, no, she's not on drugs," I assured him. "That I know of. She's just had a rough week."

"You're done." Rich moved in with a pair of gigantor security guards. "I'll need your set pass right now."

"Here! Choke on it!" Jacinda flung her set pass at Rich and gathered up her purse and street clothes. She peeled off her sweater and skirt in full view of the lighting and camera crews. "This is bullshit. This outfit is bullshit, this show is bullshit, and I hope you get cancelled in May."

She stepped out of the ballet flats and into her wedge-heeled espadrilles, then strutted off toward the parking lot like Cleopatra in a fluttery black miniskirt and a push-up bra.

For several seconds, there was dead silence. Then Caitlin asked me, "She's your roommate, right?"

"Her?" I blinked. "No. I barely know her. We just met."

Rich pulled a roll of chewable antacids out of his pants pocket and downed a few of the chalky white tabs. "That's a wrap for today, people. We'll regroup tomorrow at eight A.M."

Everyone was casting speculative glances at me and murmuring about "those Allora girls." I slunk over to the row of canvas cast member chairs and tried to hide behind Teague, who appeared both amused and aroused.

"You should really get into more girl fights," he drawled. "Very hot."

"This is going to make the tabloids, you know," I said miserably. "The G-Spot is going to crucify her tomorrow."

"A fate worse than death." He inhaled deeply, savoring the cool breeze blowing in from the ocean. "We have the rest of the day free and you owe me a date."

"But . . . right now?" I didn't have a perfect first-date outfit on, or my lucky earrings. Plus, I had about two inches of makeup caked on my face.

"Right now." He slung his arm around me and steered me toward his trailer.

"But what about—"

"Less talk, more action. Let's go."

9

"Are we there yet?" I stopped walking down the sun-baked asphalt path and leaned over to readjust my shoe.

"Why so impatient?" Teague grabbed my shoulder to steady me. "Didn't anyone ever tell you that getting there is half the fun?"

I grimaced at the giant red blister forming under the leather straps of my flip-flops. "Whoever said that must have been wearing sensible shoes."

Teague shook his head in exasperation. "Who wears flip-flops with *heels*, for God's sake? That's the most sadistic thing I've ever seen."

"Wedges are in this year," I replied, prodding the blister. "Besides, you shaved your head and lost twenty pounds for your role in *Shoot the Moon.*"

"Twenty-five, actually. But that was for the sake of my art. Shoes are—"

"Fashion, which is an art form in itself," I finished smartly.

"Yeah, I'm sure Old Navy's already secured their place in the Smithsonian." Teague knelt down beside me and inspected my swelling toes.

"René Caovilla is hardly Old Navy, my friend."

"Come on, then, take them off and we'll walk in the sand."

We were following the bike path that ran along the Malibu shoreline, passing boxy white lifeguard stands and the huge, gated beach houses of the rich and famous.

I slipped off the controversial shoes, then let him lead me barefoot through the warm sand to the ocean's edge. "And you still refuse to tell me where we're going?"

"We're almost there," he repeated. He had wasted no time washing off his makeup, grabbing a ball cap and sunglasses (the better to deter paparazzi and autograph hounds), and spiriting me away from the set in his car, which had turned out to be a modest black Toyota Prius. After my recent forays into L.A. dating, I'd been expecting a sporty foreign coupe or an armored SUV, so the simple sedan had come as a surprise.

"I like to stay under the radar," he'd said when I commented. "You have more options if you're anonymous."

"This from the guy who club hops like it's his second job?"

"That's another option." He put the car in neutral and playfully revved the engine like he was about to race a Lamborghini. "But when that lifestyle takes over your real life, you're screwed. Ever been up to Malibu?"

"Nope," I'd admitted, buckling my seat belt as we vroomed out of the parking garage into the blazing late-afternoon sunlight.

"Okay, then. Today we do low profile, Friday night we'll do high profile at Dice."

"Except I'm not going to Dice with you Friday night," I reminded him. "Family thing, remember?"

"Well, then, we better make today count."

So here we were, strolling along the shoreline with the blue sky and the water blurring at the edge of the horizon.

We walked so close together that my bare arm grazed

his shirt sleeve. If either of us had flexed our fingers out, we would be holding hands.

"The air smells different out here." I closed my eyes and breathed in the damp salt water. "Really clean."

"That's because all the smog and pollution is blown inland. You can see the stars at night out here, too."

Until he said that, I hadn't realized how much I missed the clear night sky I'd grown up with. In L.A., all you saw was the moon and an occasional airplane. Cloud cover and blinking neon obscured the stars, and after a while you forgot to search for them.

"It's nice to get a little breathing room." I dangled my flip-flops over the foamy waves that lapped up to our toes. "I'm sure this place is packed on weekends."

"Yeah, but I like it empty. I miss wide-open spaces."

"You grew up in Australia, right?" I tried to sound casual, like I hadn't Googled him within an inch of his life and memorized his height, middle name, and astrological sign.

"A ranch in Queensland. I'm a banana bender."

I raised my eyebrows. "What is *that?*"

He laughed at my expression. "It's someone from Queensland."

"Well, it sounds obscene!"

"Get your mind out of the gutter, girl. There's an old

joke that bananas grow straight, and we squish 'em for packing."

My eyebrows went up higher still. "So you grew up on a banana ranch?"

"Cattle ranch, actually."

"Then why . . .?"

"Why do we get stuck with banana jokes? Who knows? It's better than being a Sandgroper, though. That's someone from the west."

I shook my head. "Whatever. So what'd you do on this farm? Did you have to get up at the crack of dawn and milk cows?"

"Ranch, not farm. And we did whatever needed doing—the whole family."

"You have three brothers, right?" I asked.

"Yeah—how'd you know?"

I quickened my pace. "Uh, you told me. Yesterday, in your trailer."

"Did I?" He threw me a cagey look.

I quickly changed the subject. "So how'd you get from the land of the Banana Benders to Hollywood?"

"I'm the black sheep, so to speak. I'm never happy with staying in one spot—I always wanted to see the world."

"And here it is." I gestured to the sweeping expanse of deserted beach in front of us.

"Exactly. We didn't have a TV or high-speed Internet."

I gasped. "You didn't? But that's child abuse!"

"Not according to my mum. I liked to read, but the trouble was, we only had about twenty books. They were all old and dusty, with microscopic print. Amazon.com doesn't deliver to the back of beyond. One day I was laid up in bed, sick, and I was stone bored so I broke down and sampled a little bit of Shakespeare. After that, I was hooked. I pestered my mum to go to the theater—a real theater—until she couldn't stand it anymore and took me to a production of *As You Like It* in Brisbane."

None of the online articles I'd read had mentioned anything about Shakespeare. I'd just assumed he'd been born searingly hot and had decided to cash in on that. "So you didn't start out in television?"

"No, I did bit parts in regional productions until I was eighteen. Then I moved to New York to give Broadway a go."

"All by yourself?"

"*You* moved out here all by yourself, didn't you?"

"Yeah, but my aunt is out here. And my mom. Sort of." He waited for me to elaborate on that, but I steered the conversation back to him. "So you moved to New York to do theater. Did you work with anyone famous?"

"Not on Broadway, I didn't. I couldn't get cast to save my life. Finally, my agent told me to stop being such a bloody purist and go out for some commercials. I was down to my last dollar and rent was due, so . . ."

"Commercials." I nodded. "That's how I got my start, too."

"My first job was for some high-tech razor—you know, with the fifteen blades and all—and I had to flex my jaw and stare moodily into the camera like Heathcliff on the moors."

I was ninety-nine percent sure he was referencing *Wuthering Heights,* but I didn't want to ask and risk looking like an ignorant American, so I just smiled.

"The director on that commercial was getting ready to shoot the pilot for *Westchester County,* and he needed a tall, brooding bloke to play Jake. So here I am."

"Living the dream," I said.

"Living the dream."

"Are you sorry you never got to do Broadway?"

He shrugged. "Maybe I'll try again someday, when this is over."

I turned to face him, shading my eyes with my hand. "When what's over?"

"This." He threw out his arms to encompass the sky, the sea, the ritziest town on the West Coast. "Everything. Hollywood's a game. It's all temporary, and one of these days the machine is going to spit me back out."

I thought about my mother, about how brightly she'd burned and how quickly she'd burned out.

"How did you know I like my men bitter and cynical?" I teased.

"I'm not bitter, but I'm not stupid, either. So I might as well enjoy the ride while it lasts."

"Hence, the club hopping and bed hopping?"

He laughed. "I see my reputation precedes me."

"Let me guess: Don't believe everything I read?"

"Don't believe, period. You're in the bullshit capital of the universe."

"How reassuring."

"I won't lie—I've definitely had my share of the local girls."

I gave him a look.

"Maybe some other blokes' shares, as well," he admitted. "But they had fun, and they got what they wanted out of the deal."

"Which was what?" I put one hand on my hip. "A chance to have sex with a real, live celebrity?"

More laughter. "Who said anything about sex?"

"Like you said, your reputation precedes you."

"Fair point. But no, what they want, mostly, is to be *seen* with a real, live celebrity. Photos taken, name in the papers, all that."

"And the fact that you're rich and good-looking has nothing to do with it?"

He pounced. "You think I'm good-looking?"

"We're not talking about me," I blustered. "We're talking about you and your endless parade of girl-friends."

"I told you, they're not girlfriends. They're mostly interested in going to premieres and meeting my agent."

"They use you, you use them, and everyone goes on their merry way? That is *so* romantic."

"It's not like that," he protested. "I told you, everything here is temporary. Someday I'll move back to Oz, buy a big ranch, and get back to real life, but until then . . ."

"Just fun," I summed up. "No strings."

"Exactly. Enjoy responsibly, as the liquor commercials say. I'm always on the road, doing too many projects at once. I'm no good to anybody long-term."

I started walking again. "Then what are we doing here?"

"We're living in the moment."

"Yeah. I'm not really known for living in the moment."

"Then now's your chance to learn." He rested his hand on the small of my back and urged me forward. "Don't worry about what happens next."

I had to laugh because, come on. *Don't worry?* That was like asking me to stop breathing.

"This . . ." I gestured back and forth between us. "Whatever this is, it isn't going to work."

"Maybe not." He seemed totally unfazed. "We'll see."

"I'm a virgin." I blurted this out before I could think, and clapped my hands over my mouth.

He just nodded. "Good to know."

"Well, so the whole 'just fun, no strings thing' . . . I can't do that."

We skirted an outcropping of craggy rocks, then Teague pointed toward a gray-shingled, weather-beaten shack tucked behind a public bathroom. "Okay, we're here."

"That's why we've been walking for hours? I got this ginormous blister for a dilapidated *shack?*"

"Not just any shack. Come on." He towed me toward the ramshackle building, which, upon closer inspection, boasted a sagging front porch, peeling white paint, and a driftwood sign reading GROG over the front door.

"Grog?" I laughed. "As in 'yo ho ho and a bottle of rum'? How is this place in Malibu?"

"It's the crown jewel of Malibu." Teague sounded proud. "Only a very select few know about it. The shabby chic façade keeps out the riffraff."

The porch creaked ominously under our weight. I peered through the screen door. "You got my back if we get in a bar brawl with Captain Hook, right?"

"Absolutely."

The bar's interior pretty much matched the exterior—low ceilings, splintery wooden beams, and no frills whatsoever. But there was a massive stone fireplace at one end of the room, flanked on either side by built-in shelves, which held an impressive selection of paperback books. The opposite wall consisted of a varnished, beer-stained counter and a huge picture window. The view was unbelievable.

"Did this used to be someone's house?" I asked as Teague headed for the bar.

"Probably." Teague made eye contact with the bartender, who looked spectacularly unimpressed to have a celebrity in the house. "I never asked. That's the great thing about this place—no one bothers me, and I return the favor."

Other than the bartender, Teague and I had the bar to ourselves (well, it *was* only three in the afternoon) and I started to enjoy the absurdity of a dive bar tucked in amidst the most expensive real estate in the world.

"I'll have a Victoria Bitter," Teague said, then turned to me. "And for you?"

"Um . . ." I didn't like beer, and no way was I about to drink the hard stuff on a first date with a guy like Teague. That was just asking for trouble. Besides, what if I got carded?

"What?" Teague raised an eyebrow. "What's with the face?"

"What face?"

"It's not an algebraic theorem, it's just a drink."

"Well . . ." Why oh why couldn't I escape my inner Goody Two-shoes? "You're not going to let me get away with just iced tea, are you?"

He looked insulted. "What is that supposed to mean? You think I want to get you drunk?"

"We *are* in a bar . . ."

"Let me tell you something, lovely. I don't need alcohol to close the deal with a girl."

I flushed from the roots of my hair to the soles of my feet.

"Don't have a beer on my account. You can't resist me even when you're sober."

"But—"

"She'll have an iced tea," Teague told the bartender. After he paid and collected our frosty glasses, he led me over to a pair of wobbly stools by the picture window. "There you are. Cheers."

I clinked my glass against his. "Cheers. And by the way, I *can* resist you."

"Whatever you say."

We sipped our drinks in silence for a few moments, watching the white caps roll in. I stopped obsessing about everything and just savored the view.

He was first to break the silence. "You haven't told me anything about yourself. You must be bored to tears, listening to me bang on about Shakespeare and banana benders. What about you? Where did you grow up? What's your family like?"

I considered telling him the truth. For about five nanoseconds. Then I smiled and said, "You know what? The whole just-fun, no-strings idea is starting to grow on me. And if this is just fun, you don't need to know my whole life story. Less history, more mystery."

He laughed. "You're an unusual girl."

"That's what they tell me."

"Hey." He nodded out at the expanse of ocean. "If we could go anywhere right now, anywhere in the world, where would you want to go?"

If I'd been out to prove how exotic and adventurous I was, I'd have said Antarctica or Côte D'Ivoire or outer

Mongolia. But I was sick of pretending to be sophisticated.

"Venice." When I was little, my mother had sent me postcards from a fashion shoot she'd done there. I'd carried the photos of canals and cobblestone courtyards around in my pocket until my grandmother accidentally put them through the wash. I'd promised myself that when I grew up, I'd see Italy for myself. I'd see everything that my mom had written about—I wouldn't have to make up stories based on the maddeningly short sentences scribbled in her careless cursive. "Unoriginal but true."

"Venice is beautiful," Teague said. "You'd love it. We'll have to go."

"Sure." I rolled my eyes. "Then we'll hit Paris and Madrid."

He leaned over and murmured into my ear. "I promise you'd have a good time. Bella Santorini would go, you know."

My inner Bella Santorini was already packing her bags and putting on perfume and decadent lingerie. Once I let her out, I knew there'd be no stopping her, and that's what I was afraid of.

# 10

"We need to do something about Jacinda," I told Coelle on Friday afternoon while I got prepped for the big dinner with my mom and my half brother. "She's self-destructing before our eyes."

"That's because she's self-destructive." Coelle glanced up from today's literary masterpiece: *Pride and Prejudice.* "Duh."

"I know, but she's taken it to a whole 'nother level.

She got fired from *Westchester County.* The director gave her the boot in front of the whole crew."

"What'd she do? Steal his boyfriend?"

"Coelle. This is serious."

"Hey, it's a legitimate question."

"She had a flaming meltdown. Screamed at Caitlin Hoffman, screamed at the director, threatened me with bodily harm, and stripped down to her undies out in broad daylight." I wriggled into a black-and-white-patterned wrap dress and tied the sash in a jaunty bow.

"Hmm." Coelle went back to her book. "Sounds like business as usual."

"Business as usual is having too many kir royales at a club and throwing up in the men's bathroom. Or 'accidentally' pulling a nip slip on the red carpet. But this was different. She wasn't doing it to get attention—"

"Ha. That girl does *everything* to get attention."

"No, I mean it. I think . . . I know this sounds crazy, but I think part of what pushed her over the edge was that wardrobe had dressed her up in this prissy pink outfit."

"So?"

"So she looked just like her sister. It was freaky; they could've been twins. And you know how she feels about Pemberley."

"An interesting theory." Coelle turned a page. "But ultimately not my problem."

I marched across the carpet in the to-die-for pair of black suede slingbacks I'd borrowed from Jacinda's closet (she'd never miss them) and plucked the book out of Coelle's hands.

"Grow up," I snapped. "It's time for you to get over yourself and rejoin the real world."

Coelle grabbed for the novel, but I dangled it out of her reach. "I *am* grown up," she said icily. "I'm the only one in this apartment who is! You know, I had to sit through a lot of therapy over the last thirty days, and I did a lot of thinking about which of my so-called friends are dead weight. And Jacinda Crane-Laird? Is a psychological anvil."

"What did you say to me when I first got here and Jacinda was hazing the crap out of me and you needed someone to get her to go to the free clinic?"

Coelle clamped her mouth shut and smoldered.

"You said Jacinda didn't have a lot of friends."

"That's right. Because she's a—"

"Hang on a second. You convinced me to help her. Even though she'd be pissed. Even though I wanted to kill her for everything she'd done to screw up my life."

Coelle looked to be about thirty seconds away from physically tackling me to the ground and wrestling her book out of my grasp. She could take me, too—that girl hit the gym every single day. "Last month, when Jacinda called Laurel and your mom on you, she was trying to do the right thing. Even though she knew you'd be furious. Because she's your friend."

"Fine." Coelle folded her arms. "So we're even."

"That's it?" I handed back the book, then fastened a pair of flashy faux ruby studs into my earlobes. "You're just going to give up on her when she needs you?"

"Someday she's going to find out that she can't treat the whole world like her toilet," Coelle snitted. "The whole poor-little-rich-girl routine is played out."

"So you won't help me?"

"There's nothing to help you with," Coelle countered. "The girl has been on a collision course with chaos since the day she set foot in Los Angeles."

"But her sister—"

"Is her problem." Coelle gave me a stern look to indicate that this was her final word on the subject. "Now stop lecturing me and stand still—your hair looks like a rat's nest in the back."

"I was trying to tease it."

"You failed miserably. Here—let me do it. What are you all gussied up for anyway? Hot date?"

My mind flashed to the stolen afternoon I'd shared with Teague in Malibu, but I wasn't ready to share the details with anyone.

"I wish," I said casually. "No, it's a family dinner with my mom and my brother. She begged us to do it and you know what that means."

"Oh boy." Coelle made a face. "Here we go again."

"Exactly. You'd think I'd learn, but nope."

"You need an intervention more than Jacinda does."

"Your roommate seems nice," Thomas said as we hurried into Café Ramona, ten minutes late.

"She is. Coelle's the normal one," I said as the hostess led us out to the garden patio adjoining the restaurant's main dining room. "Wait till you meet my other roommate, Jacinda: she's like the second coming of Paris Hilton."

"Thomas! Eva! My darling, darling babies!" My mother scraped back her wrought-iron chair, got to her feet, and started gushing so loudly that every other diner stopped talking and stared at us. "Look at the two of you together." She clasped her hands over her chest. "You're so beautiful it breaks my heart."

Thomas looked mortified.

She flung out her arms for a hug. "Evie! Sweetpea!"

I stared at her, my mouth open. "Oh my God, what did you do to your hair?"

"You like it?" Her long, wavy black hair, the "signature feature" that she spent hours styling and conditioning with a top-secret mixture of oils from the Brazilian rain forest that cost hundreds of dollars per ounce, had been dyed blonde. And I'm not talking highlights. I'm talking, full-on, no-turning-back, root-to-tip platinum.

"I . . . yeah, actually." My mom and I shared the same olive skin tone, so she should look awful as a blonde. "Should" being the operative word. She must have paid some crafty colorist a fortune, because she looked drop-dead gorgeous. What the hell? No matter how much she drank or smoked or made terrible hair color choices, she still looked like the twenty-two-year-old supermodel she'd been in the eighties. Maybe this went beyond a plastic surgeon and a colorist—maybe she'd struck a deal with the devil.

I made a mental note to ask Coelle if she'd researched anything about Satanic bartering for her newest role. "Why the sudden change? Let me guess—you and Tyson broke up? Again?"

My mother shot Thomas a pointed look. "You see? She always has to attack me. I try to be nice, but she won't let me. Didn't I tell you?"

Thomas glanced at me, glanced back at our mother, then stared fixedly down at his menu.

"Anyway—" Mom turned back to me "—yes, as a matter of fact, I did get rid of Tyson. For good, this time.

He was nothing but a stuffy, pompous boor with a bank-book where his heart should be."

"Really." I tried to keep the skepticism out of my voice.

"Yes, *really*. You don't have to be snotty about it—I do have standards, you know." Mom checked her reflection in a polished butter knife.

"Since when?"

"Eva Cordes!" She slammed the knife back down on the table. "That is *enough!*"

The well-groomed, elderly couple at the next table stood up, tossed down their napkins, and escaped to the indoor dining room, muttering all the way about "young ladies these days" and "shockingly rude."

"And . . . cut." I pantomimed clapping down a director's slate board. "Okay, we've physically driven people away. I think we're ready to move on and get down to business."

Thomas looked like he'd give anything to be back home in Sherman Oaks, having a nice, normal dinner with his nice, normal family.

"It's okay," I reassured him. "This happens every time."

"You are so difficult," my mother hissed. As she crossed her legs, I noticed she was wearing black leather pants. And a tailored white shirt unbuttoned far enough so the whole world could see she hadn't bothered with a bra. And enough gold jewelry to replenish Fort Knox.

"Someday you'll be sorry you were so heartless to me. Someday. Wait and see."

"So, Mom." I leaned forward and cocked my head in the posture I'd seen Aunt Laurel adopt when she was getting ready to wheel and deal. "What can we do for you?"

"We haven't even ordered yet," she replied stiffly.

"I know, but you said you wanted to turn over a new leaf. So let's be honest with each other for a change, what do you say? Just this once?"

Her face sagged. For a moment, I could see the age lines creeping in around her forehead and mouth. "You're never going to stop hating me, are you?"

Thomas made a muffled, strangling noise deep in his throat.

"I don't hate you," I said, and it was true. I wanted to hate her; I'd *tried* to hate her for years and years, but somehow hope always trumped the anger in my heart. I couldn't quite give up on her, even though I knew I should.

"What about you?" She turned to Thomas, dabbing dramatically at her eyes under the sunglasses. "I suppose you hate me, too?"

"I . . . uh . . ." He tugged at the collar of his blue polo shirt.

"Or are you utterly indifferent to me?" She sighed. "You have a new family now. I suppose you don't even think of me as your mother." More dabbing.

"Hey, leave him out of this." I planted both elbows on the table, shielding my brother from her.

"All I want is to know that my son loves me. Is that so wrong?"

"When you gave him up as a baby and never even called? *Yes*!"

"It wasn't that simple!" she cried. "Maybe you can't understand that, Eva, but Thomas does. *Thomas*—"

"Stop! Don't suck him into this black hole of dysfunction, okay?" I knew that technically Thomas was the older sibling, but I couldn't help defending him. I'd had years of practice deflecting my mother's mind games. He was fresh meat. "He still has a chance to lead a relatively nonscrewed-up life. So let him go, Mom. Let him go."

"Hey." Thomas nudged me aside. "I can take care of myself."

"Don't engage," I advised him. "It'll only make things worse."

"I've changed!" My mom reached across the table for my hand, her gold bracelets jangling. "I know you don't believe me, but it's true!"

I got to my feet. "Come on, Thomas, we're leaving."

Mom seized my brother's forearm with both hands. "You can't go!"

"Oh, we're going." I smoothed the skirt of my black dress. "Come, on, T." I'd never called him that before, but it seemed to fit. Brothers and sisters had nicknames for each other, right?

"T" remained in his chair, trapped in the battle of wills. When he shifted toward me, my mom sank her fingernails into his skin and wailed piteously.

"Wait!" she keened. "I need you! I need you both!"

"For what?" I demanded.

"For my big comeback."

I folded my arms over my chest. "Oh boy. Here we go."

She knew that her ploys for sympathy would cut no ice with me, so she focused her efforts on Thomas. "It's been rough breaking back into the business. I've made a few enemies over the years—not my fault, of course—"

"Don't even try to blame this on my father!" I exclaimed. "The man has been dead for eighteen years!"

"He blacklisted me, Eva. More to the point, his ancient gorgon of a wife blacklisted me, and she hobnobs with a lot of influential people. I need a really great project to launch me back into the stratosphere. I've got the raw materials: beauty, brains, talent out the yin-yang. But I need the right vehicle. And I've finally found it." She took a deep breath. "You are looking at the next reality superstar."

Thomas grabbed his water glass and chugged.

"Mom!" I gasped. "No! Not reality TV. There are *limits!*"

She sat up straight, glowing with pride. "The network wants to do a show called *Model Material.* I thought up the title—catchy, right? The concept is *America's Next Top Model* meets *The Swan.* Very edgy, very now. We're going to choose sixteen homely, insecure girls from all over America, and I'm going to groom them into model material. I'll teach them all about style, nutrition, dating . . . and by the end of the show, their whole lives will have changed."

"Marisela Cordes, patron saint of glam," I scoffed.

"Exactly! I'm going to take the poor creatures under my wing and mentor them. Mother them."

"Hold up." I sat back down at the table. "You're going to *mother* them?"

"Mm-hmm." She pulled out a compact and powdered her nose.

"And you want us to help you?"

"Mm-hmm."

"And you don't see the irony here?"

She blinked. "What irony, baby?"

"Never mind."

"The show is going to debut in January as a mid-season replacement for some sucky police drama that everybody knows is doomed, and the network wants to start drumming up interest as soon as possible. I've been out of the spotlight for quite a while, but I know how to sell myself. So what we're going to do is—"

"Hang on." Thomas finally recovered the power of speech. "Who is 'we,' exactly? What are we supposed to do?"

She cleared her throat daintily. "Eva and I . . . well, there have been a few items in the press that don't exactly make me out to be mother of the year. And when they find out about you, Thomas, which they will—never underestimate the power of the media—there may be some libelous gossip about me being a bad role model."

"Those damn tabloids," I said dryly. "Always stretching the truth."

"I know! Luckily, I know how to beat them to the punch."

My stomach lurched.

"That's where you two come in. We're going to do an interview—all together—and explain the truth about our family."

"What kind of interview?" Thomas asked at the same moment I asked, "What kind of truth?"

Mom tossed her head, her dangly earrings catching the fading sunlight. "We're going to sit down with Remy Johansen for the exclusive Cordes family tell-all. Primetime. A full hour."

Remy Johansen was the Gen-X version of Diane Sawyer: soft-spoken and sweet on the surface, but not afraid to ask the hard questions. Questions like, "Do you really consider your mother your best friend?" and "If your father were alive today, Eva, what would you say to him?"

"You want us to go on live TV and lie?" I asked.

"I'm not going on TV," Thomas said flatly.

Mom's smile vanished for a second, but then it blinked right back on, brighter than before. "First of all, darling, everyone wants to be on TV."

"I don't." Thomas sat back with a mulish expression.

"Of course you do! It's the American dream."

"Not mine."

She opened her mouth, shut it, and turned to me. "And no one's asking you to *lie,* baby girl. We're going to tell the truth: that we're a fractured, unconventional, but loving family that somehow works despite all odds."

Thomas was firmly in my camp now. *"This* works?"

"I warned you," I said smugly. "Didn't I warn you?"

"We'll meet with a team of PR professionals beforehand, of course, just to make sure we're all on the same page—"

"So we can practice lying about how much we all adore each other," I translated.

"Stop this right now, both of you!" She stomped her designer ankle boots in frustration. "I am trying to do what's best for us all and you are just being ungrateful brats! You are going to do this interview and you are going to like it!"

I slung my bag over my shoulder. "Are we done?"

Thomas scraped back his chair. "We're done."

"Let's go." We sped toward the exit while my mother yelled after us, "But we're supposed to have dinner! You promised!"

The ride back to my apartment was blissfully free of awkward silences. We chattered away as if we'd known each other our whole lives, both of us interrupting with "She's crazy" and "I *know!*"

Finally, my brother and I had something to talk about.

# 11

"Bonding" with my mother always left me frazzled, defensive, and shell-shocked, so I was looking forward to a quiet night in front of the TV with a pizza and a chocolate milkshake from In-N-Out. If only. My fantasies of peace and quiet lasted less than fifteen minutes. I walked through the apartment's front door to find Jacinda on her hands and knees in the living room, rooting through piles of magazines and cast-off couture while screaming, "Where is my red lip gloss?"

"Hi honey, I'm home," I said to her red-velvet-clad booty. "Can I help you with something?"

"You stole my lip gloss, didn't you? How many times have I told you: Keep your grimy paws off my shit!"

I was too distracted by her outfit to respond to her accusation. "Good lord, girl. What are you *wearing?*"

She struggled to her feet and struck a pose to show off her skimpy, strategically shredded velvet dress, black patent pumps, and fishnet stockings. "You like? Pemberley's having an engagement party tonight."

"I thought you said fishnets make you spontaneously combust."

"They're just the tip of the iceberg." She showed off her blood-red manicure, thick black eyeliner, and a brand-new serpent tattoo on her chest.

"Tell me that's temporary," I said.

"Of course it is. I would never besmirch my perfect boobs with anything so tacky as a reptile. But don't tell Pemberley that—it'll ruin the effect. Now, I'm only going to ask you this once more: What did you do with my red lip gloss?"

"I didn't touch your lip gloss," I snapped. "And you shouldn't show up to your sister's engagement party looking like a hooker on the Sunset Strip."

"Let me tell you something about my sainted sister— she didn't even *invite* me to her precious party." Jacinda's smile was vicious. "She's ashamed of me. So I'm going to give her something to be ashamed *about.*"

"You're crashing your own sister's engagement party?"

"As soon as I finish my makeup. You want to come?"

"I'm not sure this is really the best idea," I hedged as Jacinda strode to the kitchen and pulled two boxes of wine out of the cupboard. "Since when do you drink wine out of a box?"

"I'm not going to drink it." She made a face at the very idea. "I'm giving one box to the happy couple. The other box I'm wearing. This is my signature scent tonight—eau de cheap vino." She punched a hole in the top of one box with a paring knife and splashed some red wine on her dress.

"Come on. Don't do this."

"Too late. It's done. And if I can't find the red lip gloss, I'll have to go with my backup: black."

She jingled her car keys in my face, waltzed across the living room, and headed outside. As I watched her go, Coelle's word echoed through my mind: *The girl has been on a collision course with chaos since the day she set foot in Los Angeles. There's nothing you can do to help her.*

Then I grabbed the keys to the Goose and ran out after her.

* * *

I had no trouble following Jacinda—her little silver convertible stood out from the crowd of sedans and SUVs on the streets, and the Goose's hulking size provided excellent windshield visibility. After twenty minutes of stop-and-go traffic on Santa Monica Boulevard, the convertible turned down a quiet side street. I followed her to Claude, an exclusive, upscale restaurant that my aunt had informed me catered to the snootiest of the snooty.

When Jacinda saw me pull up to the valet stand behind her, she threw her keys at the parking attendant and yelled. "Get out of here, Cordes! You and this rusty monstrosity of a car are an embarrassment!"

"I'm just trying to save you from yourself."

"Eva of Arc. You're such a little angel, you make me physically ill." She gagged. "Well, what the hell. As long as you're here, you might as well see the fireworks. Let's go." She grabbed my arm and dragged me toward the restaurant.

"Jacinda, wait. I know you're mad at Pemberley, but this isn't—"

"Shut it." She stormed toward the front doors.

"Wait!" I dug in my heels and pulled her back.

She paused for a moment, looking surprised. "You

can't stop me," she said. "No one can. And by the way—" her gaze flicked over the casual black-and-white dress I'd worn for my family dinner—"that outfit is inappropriate for this venue."

"Look who's talking."

When a man at the restaurant's entrance blocked our path and informed us, "I'm terribly sorry, but we're closed tonight for a private party," Jacinda replied in a loud voice, "I'm with the bride" and strutted right past.

We burst into the dining area, which was a high-ceilinged room decorated in minimalist florals. The pale green walls had orchids silk-screened on them in black ink, and each table featured a single orchid centerpiece surrounded by several square silver candles. Waiters in crisp white dress shirts and black ties passed silver trays laden with champagne and appetizers.

"The entertainment has arrived," Jacinda announced, sticking out one hip and licking her lips.

The guests, all of whom looked like they'd been teleported directly out of *Vogue*'s "People and Parties" column, turned to gape at us.

"Jacinda!" Pemberley swooped down on us, wearing a violet strapless dress that almost matched the color that her face turned when she saw her sister's outfit. "What on earth are you doing here?"

"Well, you *are* my sister," Jacinda said, again much louder than necessary. "I knew you'd want me here."

"I do *not* want you here and this is why. Look at you! Good heavens, you're . . ." Pemberley broke off and started sniffing. "Have you been *drinking?*"

"All night," Jacinda answered. "And I got another tattoo—look!"

For a second, I thought Pemberley was going to faint dead away. Then she straightened her shoulders, closed one hand around Jacinda's elbow and the other around mine, and marched us in lockstep to the alcove by the restrooms. I thought I heard someone call my name as I retreated, but when I glanced over my shoulder, I didn't see anyone I recognized.

"I cannot believe you," Pemberley quavered, her blue eyes brimming with tears. "This is my special night, everyone I care about is here, and you have to ruin it for me! Chip is from a good family—a *respectable* family. What are his parents going to say when they see you like this? What are Mother and Daddy and going to say?"

Jacinda's eyes got huge. "Mom and Dad are here?"

"Yes! They flew in to surprise me! And now—"

"Well, why didn't they tell me they were coming?"

Pemberley threw up her hands. "Why would they? Honestly, we can't take you anywhere. Someday, when you finally grow up, you're going to realize that—"

"Pem?" An oily male voice oozed into our conversation. "What's the matter, kitten?"

Pemberley stifled a little squeak as Chip ambled into the hall. "Nothing, darling. Everything's fine. Why don't you keep mingling with the guests and I'll just—"

Too late. "You must be Jacinda." Chip, who was shorter and stockier than I'd imagined after seeing him in his sports car, gave my roommate a thorough once-over. She stiffened but stared right back at him. "Nice dress, honey, but it's not that kind of party."

Pemberley covered her eyes with her hands. "She was just leaving."

"So you're the Crane-Laird daughter no one will talk about." As Chip came closer, I could smell cigar smoke embedded in his tailored black suit. Silver cuff links glinted at his wrists. "It's nice to finally lay eyes on you."

The way he looked at Jacinda made me uncomfortably sure that he must have viewed her infamous topless Internet photos. Multiple times. But she ignored the ogling, held out her right hand. and said, "Charmed," in a cultured voice that would have been better accompanied by a curtsey.

"Hey, the pleasure is all mine." He shook her hand and held on until she wormed free of his grasp.

"Jacinda! What in heaven's name are you doing here?"

We all whipped around to face a slender, middle-aged woman and a white-haired, elderly man. The woman looked coolly elegant in a black silk sheath dress with a pearl-and-sapphire necklace, and her hair was chestnut brown. I could see an unmistakable family resemblance in her green eyes and angular cheekbones. She had to be Jacinda's mother. As for the old guy . . .

"Oh, Daddy!" Pemberley threw herself into his arms, nearly shoving him through the kitchen doors. "She's ruined my special night!"

"What? Eh?" Daddy looked confused. Apparently, his hearing wasn't the best.

"Now, now, kitten." Chip patted Pemberley's shoulder. "There's no need to cry."

"But all our guests and the photographers and your parents, Chip, oh, your parents! They'll all see her like this and . . . my life is over, do you hear me? *Over!*" She buried her face in her father's charcoal gray suit jacket and sobbed.

Jacinda didn't look quite so bold and brash anymore. She slunk back into a shadowed corner with her head hung low.

The woman in black narrowed her eyes and thinned her lips. "Pemberley, this is neither the time nor the place for your theatrics. You're a grown woman, about to be married, now act like it. Stop sniveling, dry your eyes, and go back to your guests. Immediately."

Pemberley straightened up, accepted the tissue her mother offered, and took a few wobbly steps back toward the dining room.

"Go!" Her mother ordered. "You're being terribly rude."

Pemberley scurried off.

The old man looked at us, bewildered. "What's going on? Jacinda, when did you get here?"

"Oh, Heath, do stop babbling. Go with Pemberley." The dictator in bias-cut silk nudged dear old Daddy down the hall after his daughter.

Then she turned to face Jacinda, and swear to God, my blood froze in my veins. Even Chip sucked in his breath.

"*What* are you wearing and why are you here?"

Jacinda mumbled something unintelligible under her breath.

"Excuse me, I am speaking to you. What are you wearing and why are you here?"

"I didn't know you and Dad were going to be here," Jacinda finally said.

"That does not answer my question." Jacinda's mother reached into her black sequined clutch, pulled out a pair of peach oval pills, and tossed them into her mouth, dry-swallowing like a seasoned junkie. She reminded me of someone . . . but who?

I edged toward the doorway, trying to escape unnoticed, but Jacinda's mom stopped me with a single accusatory glance. "And who, may I ask, are you?"

*Daphne Farnsworth.* That's who she reminded me of. Her subzero hauteur was eerily similar to that of my dead father's wife. They were probably BFF. Daphne was probably boozing it up in the next room right now.

"I'm, uh, I'm Eva Cordes," I stammered, trying not to show fear and failing miserably. "I'm Jacinda's roommate. I mean, friend. I mean—"

"I see." She stepped toward me, and I could see her muscles tense beneath her dress. "Are you the one who's been leaking stories about my daughter to the press?"

"What? No!" I flattened my back against the wall.

"Leave her alone, Mother." Jacinda wrapped both arms around herself and rejoined the conversation. "She's not like my friends from boarding school, okay? She came here to stop me."

"Well, she didn't do a very good job of it, did she?"

"Don't blame her; it's my fault." Jacinda sighed. "I didn't know you and Daddy were going to be here."

"And if we hadn't been here, this outrageous spectacle would have been acceptable, is that what you're trying to say?"

"No, but—"

"Jacinda, we have tried with you and tried with you. If you would prefer to be invited to important family events, I suggest you start comporting yourself more like a lady and less like a drug-addled doxy."

"*I'm* drug-addled?" Jacinda regained a bit of her spitfire sass as she executed a somewhat enervated version of her signature hair toss. "Pop another Valium, Mother."

Her mother blanched. Chip looked as horrified as I felt.

"Eva?" A hand brushed my forearm, and I startled, banging my head against the wall behind me.

"Yow." Cradling the back of my skull, I turned to find Danny staring at me. Yeah. *That* Danny.

But before I could register any emotional reaction to seeing my ex, I noticed who was standing right behind him.

"Yo, yo, E! What's crackin', mamacita?"

I rubbed my eyes, but he didn't disappear.

"Why you always gotta diss me so hard, prettina? When we gonna get it poppin'?"

"This isn't happening," I whispered. "This isn't happening."

"Oh, it's happenin', shorty. Believe that! I'm a true playa for realz!"

Danny angled his shoulder forward to block me from C Money's advances. "What are you doing here?" His voice was low, but urgent.

"What are *you* doing here?" It was weird, seeing him dressed up without his baseball cap. Practically the only time I'd seen him without it had been in bed right before we—*cease, desist, don't go there!*

"Chip's parents are friends with my stepmother," Danny explained, looking everywhere but into my eyes. "So I, uh . . ."

"That's right, and y'all better recognize!" C Money howled, prompting Jacinda and her mother to put their spat on hold for a second and sneer at him with scorn. "Now you know 'sup, but it's too late for you to score a payout from my man C Money!"

I peered around Danny's shoulder. "Caleb. We meet again."

"My handle ain't Caleb, yo, it's C Money, also known as the C-Zizzle." C Money kissed his index and middle finger and then held them up in the peace sign.

I caught a glimpse of something shiny peeking out from under his suit jacket. "Tell me you're not wearing gold chains under your suit."

He grinned and pulled aside his designer tie to reveal

a gaudy, diamond-encrusted medallion engraved with an interlocking *C* and *M*.

I gave him a thumbs-up. "Nice look. Very Vegas."

"You know it, boo. The ladies like shiny stuff. They's like raccoons when it comes to the ice."

"Oh, how well you know us." I turned back to Danny. "Listen, I'm sorry. I didn't know you'd be here. I just came to—"

"I hate you!" Jacinda screamed at her mother.

"Don't make a scene!" her mother screamed back. "And what on earth is that smell? You reek of cheap wine!"

"Ladies, ladies." Chip put a calming arm around each Crane-Laird woman. "Don't upset yourselves. Louisa, go back to the party and enjoy yourself. I'll walk Jacinda back to her car—through the kitchen exit, don't worry—and everything will be fine."

Danny rolled his eyes at this, but when I shot him a questioning glance, he shook his head and refused to elaborate.

After Louisa choked back yet another peach pill and stormed off toward the dining room, Jacinda allowed Chip to shepherd her through the massive double doors to the prep kitchen. Danny and I were left to stare at each other.

Had he kissed anyone else since we broke up? Could

he tell that I'd kissed someone else? I'd moved on, I reminded myself. With a bona fide celebrity. I didn't need Danny Bristow anymore.

So why couldn't I even remember Teague's last name? (It started with an A, right? I was pretty sure.) I twisted my hands in front of me and wet my lips, trying to think of something appropriate to say.

It was impossible to tell what Danny was feeling—he looked the same as always, but older somehow. Guarded. Even though we'd only been apart a few weeks.

"I, uh . . ." I waved to Jacinda as she turned to give me a baleful, mascara-streaked stare over Chip's shoulder.

"Girl, you cold but you a dime." C Money muscled his way in between me and Danny. "Let's bounce and go chillax with some Cris, aiight?"

Danny jerked his head toward the kitchen. "I better go."

I batted my eyes at C Money. "Why don't you go order me a kir royale? I'll meet you at the bar in three minutes."

"Booyah!" He raced off toward the dining room, and I hurried after Danny.

# 12

"What was that look about?" I asked Danny as we sidestepped the sauté station in the restaurant's kitchen. The prep cooks barely looked up from their slicing and dicing. Perhaps they were used to crazy rich people using their turf as an escape route. "When Chip was talking to Jacinda's mom?"

"Chip Pettigrew went to the same prep school I did. He was a tool in high school and a he's tool now." Danny sounded disgusted.

My heel caught on a hole in the webbed rubber mat on the floor, and I pitched forward toward a rack full of pots, but Danny caught me, steadied me, and released me before I could even say thanks.

"His dad bought him admission into one of the fancy private colleges back east," Danny continued, not missing a beat. "But he had a reputation for . . . let's just say he's not a good guy."

We reached a white door emblazoned with a red exit sign and he held it open for me as we stepped into the alleyway behind the restaurant. I could hear the faint dripping of water out here, and smell the rotting produce.

"Hey." My fingers grazed his as we ventured out into the night. "I'm sorry. About Jeff. About everything, really."

He didn't say anything.

"I . . ." I wanted so badly to say "I miss you" because it was true—nothing had been the same without him— but I was afraid. He'd already walked away from me once and I couldn't bear it if he rejected me again.

So I let my voice trail off and he surprised me by filling the silence.

"I've been thinking." He sounded wary. "Since we . . . I don't know. Maybe we could—"

*Thwack!* A ringing slap echoed across the wet pavement.

"Get the hell away from me!" Jacinda yelled.

"Ow!" Chip yelled back. "You crazy little—"

There was a brief scuffle, then another slap.

"I *said,* get off me!" Jacinda sounded outraged. "Do that again and I'll break your jaw."

Danny darted into the dark corner behind the Dumpster and jerked Chip into the light pooled under the streetlamp on the corner.

"Hmph!" Jacinda was right behind them after them, straightening the hem of her dress and blotting her lipstick, which had streaked across her cheek. Danny twisted Chip's right arm up behind his back. Chip grunted, but said nothing.

"How dare you?" Jacinda jabbed her finger into Chip's chest. "You are supposed to be in love with my sister!" She reared back, made a guttural hacking noise in her throat, and spit in his face.

Chip bellowed like a wounded buffalo. "Lemme go, Bristow!"

Danny tightened his grip. "No can do. Let's go." He frog-marched Chip back toward the kitchen door.

"I'm going to tell Pemberley about this," Jacinda warned, her eyes dark with fury. "When she finds out what you did to me . . ."

"Ooh, I'm so scared," Chip sneered. "Who do you think she'll believe? The love of her life or her slutty sister?"

She launched herself toward Chip, but I managed to intervene.

"Calm down," I urged, grabbing her shoulders with both hands. "Let's not cap this night off with a trip to the emergency room."

"Forget the emergency room—that bastard's gonna need the morgue!"

"Hey." I shook her. "Stop. Breathe."

"But he— But I—"

"I know." I squeezed her arms. "But there's a time and a place. Time and a place."

"This is not over!" she warned Chip, right before Danny shoved him inside.

Jacinda wiped the last vestiges of lipstick off her cheek. "That filthy lech better sleep with one eye open because I know people, do you hear me? *I know people!* He hit on me!" She slung her gold lamé purse over her shoulder and strode toward the sidewalk. "He went way over the line. You have to believe me!"

"I believe you, I believe you." I lagged behind, watching the door Danny had disappeared through. What had he been about to say? Maybe we could *what?*

"I didn't do anything to encourage him, either." Jacinda was really getting lathered up. "I mean, I know I've had a few, like, misunderstandings with other people's boyfriends in the past, but this was my sister's fiancé! I would never—"

"I believe you," I repeated.

"But he said . . ." She frowned. "Do you really think Pemberley would take his word over mine?"

"No, of course not," I soothed. "And the sooner you tell her, the better. It's a good thing you found out about him before the wedding. Danny says—"

She pivoted and gave me a shrewd, assessing look. "Yeah, that reminds me. What the hell is Danny doing here?"

"He said his stepmom is friends with Chip's parents."

She crossed her arms. "Do not start up with him again, Eva. That's an order! He broke your heart, remember? He drop-kicked you into the depths of despair."

"I know."

"So what was up with the—" She mocked my longing look toward the door. "Haven't you learned anything? That boy is trouble."

"I know."

"And you have a hot new man, who you don't even deserve and who, if there were any justice in this miserable world, should be dating me!"

*"Yeah, yeah."*

"Well then? Stop with the wistful yearning and go bag Teague Archer."

Archer. Right. That was his last name. I knew it started with an *A*.

"Don't you have enough problems of your own without butting into mine?" I asked.

"Look." She spread out her arms and addressed the world at large. "I may be a stupid, slutty screwup, but at least I know when to let a relationship die."

"Jacinda, you're not—"

"Spare me the self-esteem pep talk, Pollyanna. I'm down to my last nerve. See you at home."

Who's that girl? Notorious ladies' man Teague Archer, in town to film a Westchester County episode, has been spotted out and about with a slender, sultry brunette. The lovebirds have been keeping a low profile, but my sources are whispering that Teague may have gotten tangled up with an ambitious newcomer with "super" genes. Watch out, Teague! This little pussycat will stop at nothing to claw her way to the top!

"What's that supposed to mean?" I shoved the Monday issue of *South of Sunset* under Coelle's nose. "Are they implying I'm just using him for his connections?"

Coelle gulped from her morning mug of green tea while she read Gigi Geltin's column for herself. "They're not implying anything—they're saying it straight out."

"Well, that's not true!" I pounded my fist on the kitchen table. "I'm suing!"

"You can't sue; it's a blind item. Besides, if you fight them on this, everyone'll know you're dating Teague."

"Yeah, but—"

"Well, I called her." Jacinda flounced down the stairs. "I told Pemberley everything that happened with Chip at the engagement party and you know what she said?"

Coelle turned up her nose and ignored Jacinda.

"What'd she say?" I asked, giving Coelle a swift kick in the shins, which she also ignored.

"She said when Chip came back to the party, he told her that *I* hit on *him!* And she believes him!"

Coelle glanced at me, and I could tell she was dying to know what had happened at the engagement party, but I wasn't about to help her out. If she wanted the dirt, she'd have to break down and talk to Jacinda.

"She said I'm a pathological liar with a narcissistic need for emotional validation." Jacinda snorted in disdain. "She reads one psych 101 textbook and she thinks she's Dr. Phil!"

"Well, did you tell her that I saw the whole thing and so did Danny and we'll back you up?" I prompted.

"No, I hung up on her." Jacinda grabbed the box of Froot Loops off the top of the fridge and poured some dry cereal straight into her mouth. "Mmph mmf mmpmmph mmph mmph."

I couldn't understand a single syllable through all that crunching. "What?"

"She said, 'Bitch can't talk to me like that,'" Coelle translated.

"Mmph." Jacinda nodded.

Coelle turned to me. "You saw Danny?"

I raised one eyebrow. "I'm telling you, you should've come with us. You missed quite a party."

Instead of unleashing another tirade about her unending wrath at Jacinda's betrayal and blah blah blah, Coelle surprised me by saying, "I had to memorize my lines. They're filming a big scene this week, and it turns out that Satan is very long-winded."

"I'm filming my big scenes this week, too," I said. "Today we do the scene where I cheat on Teague's character with Laurel's boyf—with, uh, Gavin. Hopefully, it won't be too weird." I glanced guiltily at Jacinda. "Sorry."

She swallowed her mouthful of cereal. "Why are you sorry? It's not your fault I quit."

"I thought you got fired?" Coelle pressed.

"I left to pursue other projects," Jacinda said firmly. "Creative differences, you know."

"So are you enjoying your television debut?" Coelle asked.

"Actually, it's not what I expected," I admitted. "I thought being on TV would be so exciting. But most of the time, we're just standing around waiting for them to fix the lights or fix our makeup or fix the camera angles. And learning lines was a lot harder that I thought it would be. And the early call times are killing me."

Coelle nodded. "So you don't love it?"

I nibbled my bottom lip. "I don't know. I mean, it's kind of fun when they're actually filming . . ."

"That means no," Coelle concluded. " 'Kind of fun' is not how you describe your true calling in life."

*"Absolument,"* Jacinda agreed. "If you were meant to be an actress, deep in your soul, then early call times would mean nothing."

"Excuse me?" I raised an eyebrow. "This from the girl who stripped naked and told the director she hoped his show got canceled?"

Jacinda shrugged. "I have an artistic temperament. What's your point?"

"I know that I'm not going to be in the industry forever," Coelle said, pausing to sip the last of her tea. "But I never would have made it this far if I didn't also have a passion for performing. If you don't love acting—really love it—you should quit now, because all the crap that goes with this lifestyle isn't worth it."

Aunt Laurel had said something very similar on my very first day in L.A. But if I didn't have the necessary passion for acting; if this *wasn't* my life's true calling . . . then what was?

"Don't worry," I told them with a confidence I didn't feel. "I have extreme passion for acting. Seriously. I love it."

Coelle seemed skeptical. "Have you cracked any of those books I gave you on improv and technique?"

"I skimmed them," I hedged.

She shook her head. "Dilettante. This town's full of 'em."

I changed the subject by asking Jacinda, "So what are you going to do about Pemberley and Chip?"

"What are *you* going to do about Danny and Teague?" she shot back.

"Well, girls, I'd love to stay and bicker, but I've got to go for my run. Five miles, then therapy, then filming, then class." Coelle stretched her arms over her head. "My cup runneth over."

Jacinda stopped popping pieces of cereal into her mouth. "I'll go with you."

"Running?" Coelle gathered her long, black hair into a low ponytail. "You don't run."

"I do today. Hang on two minutes—let me get changed." Jacinda bounded back upstairs.

Coelle started to yell up after her, but I shushed her. "Oh, let her go running with you."

"No way!" Coelle set her jaw. "She'll slow me down, she'll start complaining about leg cramps after two blocks, and besides, I'm still mad at her."

"Oh, give it up," I said. "You know you're not that mad anymore. And she's had a really rough time lately. Maybe we can't save her from herself, but we can be decent human beings, right?"

Coelle scowled, but she called up to Jacinda, "You can come with me, but you're not allowed to whine or pretend you're having a heart attack. We're not even going to talk, got it?"

"Fine by me," Jacinda yelled back. "There's too much talking in this apartment anyway."

After the dynamic duo laced up their sneakers and clipped on their iPods, they sprinted out the door and across the courtyard, neither saying a word. Each was obviously trying to outpace the other, but they refused to openly acknowledge any competition.

I gathered up my script, my car keys, and all the courage I could muster. Time to go make out with my jealous aunt's hunky boyfriend in front of dozens of people and my celebrity crush. Only in L. A. . . .

# 13

"Okay, this top isn't working," Stacy, the wardrobe assistant, announced. "We need something tighter—you're supposed to look busty."

"Good luck with that." I'd need duct tape, a Wonderbra, and an entire roll of toilet paper to attain that goal. But I yanked off the blue tube top and shimmied into the red-and-black halter top she handed me.

"Ooh." She winced. "No. Now your collarbone is too prominent. Maybe if we do a corset or bustier. . . . Hang on, let me see what we have left over from Meghan's fitting."

Meghan was the thin, tan blonde that the casting directors had found to replace Jacinda (not a difficult task, considering that thin, tan blondes were as common as palm trees and smog alerts out here).

Stacy hustled out the door and Teague poked his head into my (half) trailer. "Hey, lovely, got a second?"

Seeing as I was wearing only jeans and a black strapless bra, I should have been embarrassed. But he didn't comment or stare, so I decided to be daring and entertain in my underwear. "Sure. Come on in."

"Got you some coffee." He handed me a cardboard cup capped with a white plastic lid. "Tons of sugar? I took a guess."

"It's like you're reading my mind."

"Ready for the big love scene?"

"Yeah." I tried to sound nonchalant. "I mean, it's just kissing some guy I hardly know in front of a bunch of other guys I hardly know. No big deal, right?"

"Don't worry. The first time's pretty bizarre, but you get used to it."

"So you're not jealous?" I teased.

"No, but I give you fair warning that as many takes as you do with Gavin today, I'm going to make you do twice as many when we do our big love scene next week."

"Men." I sighed dramatically. "So competitive."

"Don't pretend you won't enjoy it."

"I can't believe we're going to wrap next week." I got serious. "I feel like we just started."

"That's life in the business," he said. "Easy come, easy go."

I couldn't help laughing. "Are you calling me easy?"

"No. Unfortunately. But that reminds me . . ." He gave me a slow, sexy smile. "What are your plans for next weekend?"

"Nothing, really. I told my roommate I'd help her—"

"Whatever you're doing, cancel it."

His enthusiasm was contagious. "Why?" I asked.

"Because we're going on an adventure."

"Ooh. Do tell?"

He held up his hand when I opened my mouth. "No questions. It's a surprise."

I stopped feeling nervous about the impending love scene as I tried to guess what he had up his sleeve. "Give me a little hint."

"No hints. No hints and no questions."

"You're mean."

"You're gorgeous. I like what you're wearing." He moved

in closer. I could smell faint traces of shaving cream on his cheek.

"Hey." I lowered my eyelashes and gave him the come-hither look I'd been rehearsing all week. "Do you think we should maybe rehearse a little bit?"

He brushed his lips along my jawline. "Practice makes perfect."

I was toying with the buttons on his shirt and he was toying with the back of my bra when Stacy barged back in, laden with new tops for me to try on.

"Break it up." She shooed Teague toward the door. "We have five minutes to find something to accentuate your cleavage."

"I think her cleavage is perfect as is," Teague protested, but she shut the door in his face.

"He's quite the talker, isn't he?" She handed me a ruffled gray silk number.

"And quite the kisser," I added, giggling a little.

She shook her head with the world-weary air of a behind-the-scenes veteran. "Well, have fun, but don't get too attached. These on-location flings never last."

When Stacy finally got me outfitted to her satisfaction (lacy black camisole and bra padding that would make a structural engineer proud), she sent me out to report to the director. "Gavin's already out there."

So was Aunt Laurel, who stood next to the director. You couldn't miss her prim black power suit amid the sea of jeans and T-shirts.

"Hey." I couldn't conceal my surprise. "What are you doing here? Is everything okay?"

"Everything's fine. I'm just dropping by." Her customary neutral shade of lipstick had been replaced by a sultry burgundy and her smile seemed strained. "Gavin told me your big kissing scene was today, and I thought it'd be a kick to come watch."

I died a thousand deaths inside. "You're going to be watching us? The whole time?"

"Well, sure." She smoothed back a nonexistent stray hair. "It's not every day your niece and your boyfriend go at it."

Kill me. Kill me now.

The director checked his watch. "Okay, Eva, get in the shot and let's roll. Daylight's burning."

I glanced over at Gavin, who awaited, shirtless and glistening—what *had* they slathered all over his chest?— under the lights and the boom microphone.

"Go ahead." Aunt Laurel's laugh was brittle. "This will be a hoot!"

I lowered my voice and implored her with my eyes. "There's nothing going on between me and Gavin."

"I know!" She waved me away. "Please. What, do you think I'm *jealous?*"

"I'm dating Teague Archer. Well, not dating him, exactly, it's more like a fling—"

"So I heard." Her eyebrows shot up. "The blind item in *South of Sunset* this morning wasn't exactly subtle. Well, I approve—it's an excellent career move."

I frowned. "It's not a career move."

The director was getting antsier by the second.

"You can trust me," I promised Laurel. "This is just a scene. Just acting."

"Pet, stop treating me like a halfwit and get in the damn shot."

So I did. The director yelled "action!," the cameras rolled, and Gavin did his best impression of a tortured, loyal boyfriend trying to resist temptation while I vamped around, flashing my so-called cleavage and trying to lure him into a night of cheap and tawdry sex. Thanks to Coelle's book on Method acting (which I really *had* skimmed, thank you very much), I managed to do all this without laughing and/or spontaneously combusting from embarrassment.

I slithered up to Gavin, traced the outline of his lips with my tongue (hey, it was the director's idea, not mine), and purred, "You're on vacation, so this doesn't count."

His character, being weak and male, gave in to his baser instincts and kissed me back. Then he slipped down the shoulder strap of my camisole and we "movie kissed," which was Coelle's term for smooching at unnatural angles for the camera's benefit while you moved your face around without bumping noses and tried to breathe without making any weird whistling or sniffling noises. The epitome of romance.

"Cut!" the director yelled.

Gavin and I broke apart, made eye contact, and cracked up.

"Ew! What is on your arms?" I asked, rubbing my now-slippery fingers together.

"Glycerin spray." He grinned. "I'm supposed to look sweaty."

"You feel like you just went swimming in a vat of olive oil!"

"Wardrobe!" the director yelled. "We need to fix Eva's bra! When he pulls down her top, we can see the padding."

The entire crew studied my chest, assessing the bra situation.

"Don't worry," Gavin said gallantly. "You look good. Very sexy."

"Yeah, I'm sure every guy wants to leave their girl-friend for a two-by-four in black lace." I held up my arms and tried to stand still as Stacy rushed over with pins and double-sided tape.

"Aw, come on. You're Bella Santorini," Gavin said. "Who wouldn't leave their girlfriend for you?"

That's when I noticed my aunt's face. She had dropped all pretense of casual good cheer and was standing in stony silence with her fists clenched.

"Why don't you go say hi to Laurel?" I whispered to Gavin, who had been too occupied with making sure his glycerin sweat sheen didn't have any fingerprints in it to pick up on his girlfriend's hostility.

"What?" He barely glanced up. "I'll talk to her after we finish this scene."

"She came all the way out here to see you," I urged.

"I can't handle any distractions while I'm trying to act. Believe me, if there's one person who understands putting work first, it's Laurel."

Stacy affixed a final strip of double-sided tape and proclaimed me camera-ready.

"Pull down your top," the director commanded, "Let's see how the boobs look."

I didn't even bother with the pretense of modesty, just bared my bra and posed at various angles until the camera crew decided Stacy's alterations would suffice.

"Okay, let's take it from the top. Action!"

Gavin and I ran through the scene again, after which the director declared we need to "grapple" more. "Be reluctant," he coached Gavin. "Don't give in so easily. I want to *see* the war going on between your brain and your groin!"

Then we had to do close-ups. Then we had to reshoot from four different angles. Finally, we broke for lunch.

"Okay." Gavin wiped off a layer of glycerin with a towel. "Now I'll go talk to Laurel."

But Laurel was way past the talking stage. When Gavin leaned in to kiss her cheek, she stopped him with an icy "Get over here," and dragged him off to his trailer.

I could hear the yelling from outside the flimsy metal structure. "If you want to date an eighteen-year-old, you should just say so! You don't have to humiliate me in front of all these people!"

"You're crazy!" Gavin retorted. "I *have* to kiss her! It's in the script!"

"You have to kiss her, but you don't have to be so pathetically eager about it! Even the director could tell!"

"The director was just giving me notes. What's your problem?"

"My *problem* is that you can't keep your hands off my teenage niece."

"You know what, Laurel? I can't help it if you're insecure about your age. You knew when we started going
out—"

Something hit the trailer wall with a thundering
*thump*. I flinched.

"This is not about my age!" Laurel cried indignantly.
"This is about you ogling other women every single
time we go anywhere!"

Gavin lapsed into a slow, surfer dude drawl. "The
constant jealousy, babe? I can't handle it."

"Well, you better figure out a way to handle it, buddy,
because I'm your agent!"

"Then maybe I need to find a new agent," Gavin
threatened.

"Ha! You wouldn't dare! I took you on when you
were a waiter. A waiter! I believed in you when no one
else would even glance at your head shot!"

"I'm not going to stick around like that ratty little
mutt of yours just because you got me a few auditions!"

"*Excuse* me? I'll have you know that Rhett is a pure-
bred, pedigreed poodle with champion lines going all
the way back to—"

"I don't need you or your insecurity or your snotty
little boutique agency. I quit!"

My aunt gasped. "You don't mean that."

"Yeah, I do." Gavin sounded bored with the whole

conversation. "I've been talking to some people over at TNP, and I think they might be a better fit for me. They have a vision for my career." TNP was one of the big, A-list agencies that Laurel considered her sworn enemy.

More ominous thumps from inside the trailer. "You're jumping ship to TNP? After all I've done for you!"

"Hey, don't take it personally, babe. I guess you were right—you're just too old for me."

There was a long silence. Maybe she was strangling him with her bare hands.

Finally, the trailer door squeaked open. "Fine. If this is how you want to end it, fine." Laurel sounded clipped and curt. "I wish you all the best with your new representation—filthy, unscrupulous poachers that they are—and when they chew you up and spit you out, just remember, I told you so."

"Aw, babe, don't be like that," Gavin called as she started down the steps. "It's not personal, it's just business."

"Sleeping with me isn't personal? Good to know." Laurel rounded the corner and ran right into me.

"Sorry." I shoved off the trailer's wall and tried to look like I hadn't been hanging on to every word they'd said. "I was just—"

"Evie, one of these days we are going to have to sit down and talk about respecting other people's privacy."

She straightened her blazer lapels and took a deep breath. "But, luckily for you, today is not that day."

She had her Agent Face on, betraying no emotion, but I knew she must be hurting. "I heard what Gavin said to you in there, and—"

"I don't want to discuss it." She pulled her Black-Berry out of her purse and started tapping away on the keyboard.

"Okay, but I think you should know that when we were kissing, there was really no—"

"What did I just say?" She brought her head up sharply. "It's none of your business."

But it was kind of my fault. If I hadn't had to kiss Gavin, my aunt never would have gotten upset and they never would have broken up. She had done so much for me—offered me an apartment, representation at one of the best agencies in town, a semisane adult to talk to when my mom went off the deep end—and what had I done for her? Ruined her relationship with the only boyfriend she'd had in years.

"I'm sorry," I said softly. "I really am."

"There's nothing to be sorry for," she said, but she wouldn't even look at me. "That's what I get for messing with a guy in his twenties. I should have known better."

"Well, do you want to go get coffee or something?"

I hunched my shoulders down, the better to downplay my newly manufactured cleavage. "We haven't really talked much lately."

Her cellphone rang, saving her from having to respond. "Work," she said with evident relief. "I've got to get this."

She charged off toward the parking lot, waving her arms and yelling, "Three hundred thou? That's an insult!" into the phone. So much for family bonding.

I was contemplating barging into Gavin's trailer to beat him up on my aunt's behalf when *my* cellphone rang. Thomas.

"I wanted to tell you before Marisela did," he said when I picked up. "I agreed to do that tell-all interview with her."

"But we made a pact!" I cried. "We were going to stand up to her!"

"I know." His voice was sheepish. "But she's been calling me all week, crying and . . . I don't know. I felt bad for her."

"Don't let her guilt-trip you," I admonished. "If you give in now, she'll walk all over you for the rest of your life. *Trust* me."

My brother didn't say anything.

"Thomas?"

"I can't say no."

"Yes, you can! I'll help you! Strength in solidarity, man!"

"I already told her I'd do it."

"Call her back and tell her you changed your mind."

But it was too late. My mother could be very persuasive when she wanted something. I reminded myself that my brother didn't know her the way I did. He was just an innocent bystander.

I sighed and surrendered to the inevitable. "Well, we're a team now, right? I'm not going to make you face her on national TV all by yourself. If you're in, I'm in."

# 14

"Okay, let's go over this one more time." Ashley Richman, head of Richman Public Relations and the media strategy expert my mother had hired to coach Thomas and me through the TV interview, perched on the edge of the cushy black leather sofa in Remy Johansen's greenroom. The greenroom wasn't green at all—it had been done up in black and white, with a grayish blue sectional sofa, and the whole place smelled like carpet cleaner. Ashley was the picture of polish and poise. She wore a matching olive tweed skirt and jacket with spindly-heeled brown pumps on her feet and a very strained expression on her face. Her cheeks were pale, her eyes ringed with dark half-moons of exhaustion. A week of dealing with my mother could rattle even the most battle-scarred PR pro. "Eva, if the interviewer asks you if you're resentful that your mother left you to be raised by your grandparents, you say . . . ?"

I glanced down at the notes in my hand. "I say, of course not! My mother has always been an independent free spirit, and her self-sufficiency has inspired me to pursue my own dreams."

Ashley nodded. "Good. Except you can't bring the index cards out there with you. Try to sound a little more natural, less rehearsed. Relax."

Right. Because lying through my teeth and pretending my mom was my personal hero was *sooo* relaxing.

Ashley smiled encouragingly at Thomas. "What if they ask you how you feel about your mother's promiscuity?"

Thomas, who had been programmed as thoroughly as I had, answered in a flat, robotic monotone: "Marisela is not promiscuous. She is very loving and passionate, and I feel lucky to have her in my family. Tabloids and gossip columns can say whatever they want, but Eva and I know the truth: She is a genuine, generous role model."

"Good, but I'm not feeling the sincerity," Ashley fretted.

"That's because there isn't any," Thomas said. "The woman's a nut job and we all know it."

"And she *did* kind of get around in the eighties," I chimed in. "The tabloids didn't make that up."

Ashley straightened her shoulders, all business. "Listen, kids, whatever personal grievances you may have with your mother are just that—personal. National TV is not the place to air your dirty laundry. We've been over this a hundred times: focus on the positive. You don't owe Remy Johansen anything—she doesn't care about you, she just wants a juicy story for her viewers. A little white lie here and there doesn't matter. Your loyalty should be with your mother because you love her."

Thomas and I exchanged a look.

"Right?" Ashley prompted.

"Yeah," I admitted grudgingly. "But I don't know why you're yelling at us—"

The tight little smile reappeared. "Oh, Eva, I'm not *yelling* at you—"

"Besides, we're not the ones you have to worry about," I pointed out. "We're here on time and ready to go, but where's Mom?"

"I'm here, I'm here." My mother burst into the room, a vision in blonde hair and a black velvet coat. "I know I'm late, but my hairstylist took for freaking ever doing my roots this morning and traffic was beastly."

"No problem," Ashley said smoothly. "I was just going over our talking points with Eva and Thomas. The production assistant says they want you on in ten minutes, so I better go find the makeup artist."

"Those hacks? Please." Mom made a beeline for the bathroom. "I do my own makeup. Between my runway work and the cover shoots, I've forgotten more than most of these so-called artists ever knew." She blew a pair of air kisses in our general direction. *"Mwah! Mwah!"* Hi, darlings! Are you excited?"

"Um . . ." Thomas started.

"No," I finished.

"Me, too!" She brushed liquid foundation onto her forehead with lightning speed. "We're going to get so much press out of this—we'll probably make the cover of *People*! Our family is so nontraditional and 'now.' And it doesn't hurt that we're all go gorgeous!"

"No." Ashley smiled. "That doesn't hurt at all."

"Isn't this fun?" Mom moved on to blush and eyeshadow.

Thomas narrowed his eyes and scowled.

"Hey, at least you get to go home to a real family

after this travesty is over," I whispered. "I only have my roommates, and they're as bad as she is!"

Jacinda and Coelle had officially struck a truce. That run the other morning had really galvanized Jacinda—she'd gotten up every day since and gone jogging of her own free will, thus violating both her rule about waking before noon and her rule about cardio being hopelessly pleb and passé. She'd suddenly started going to bed before midnight. I'd even caught her with a bowl of Coelle's granola this morning, but when I'd asked her what was up with the new health regimen, she had smiled and said, "Chaos is starting to get boring." Then she'd downed a chocolate croissant and a Red Bull, which I'd found oddly reassuring.

Ashley got to her feet and tapped her tasteful gold watch. "Okay, I'll be out in the studio if you need me."

"We won't," Mom trilled. "It's sweet of you to stay, though."

"Oh, I insist. It's always wise to have your publicist on hand in case the questions start getting, ahem, too far afield."

"I'm not worried," Mom said. "Kids, are you worried?"

"Yes," Thomas and I chorused.

The door closed behind Ashley, and Mom froze,

midmascara application. "Don't be silly. Why are you worried?"

"I hate being on camera," Thomas said.

"I hate talking about my childhood," I added.

"I hate my stepmom hearing me tell everyone she's not my real mom."

"I hate everyone reminding me that my dad was a total a-hole who didn't want his name on my birth certificate."

"Well . . ." Mom's face crumpled. "I don't exactly love talking about all that, either."

"We know, we know." I got up, crossed the room, and patted her on the back. "Don't cry." If she started to cry, we'd never get out of here. "Even though we don't want to talk about all that, we're going to anyway. Because we love you."

Thomas walked up next to me. "Yeah. We, uh, love you."

"So finish putting on your makeup on and let's go be the perfect family," I urged. Thomas and I smiled and for that moment, as we gazed into the mirror, we really did look like the ideal, All-American family.

"Where's that *People* photographer when we need him?" Thomas teased.

For some reason, this made my mom start crying in earnest. Not the fake, theatrical sobs she broke out when she wanted to get her way—these were fat, silent tears that streaked her makeup and made her look frightened and helpless.

"What's wrong with me?" She shook her head. "What am I doing?"

"We're doing a family interview!" Thomas gave her a little shake. "We're supposed to be happy."

"Come on, pull yourself together! Remember what Ashley says: Image is everything."

Mom buried her face in her hands. "What am I doing to my children? What am I doing to my life?"

Thomas and I made eye contact in the mirror. I don't know which of us was more freaked out. "Seriously, Mom, we're *all* fine," I said. "Just hold it together for one more hour, okay?"

There was a rap on the door. "Everybody ready?" A perky production assistant wearing headphones peeked in.

"Almost," I stammered. "We're having a moment."

"It's a very emotional time," Thomas threw in. "The three of us together after all these years."

Remy Johansen, in all her blonde, buttoned-up glory, appeared behind the production assistant. "Is there a problem?"

"Yes." Mom got to her feet and made a stand in front of the cluttered makeup table. "I can't live with these lies any longer."

"Mom, *no!*" I hissed, but Remy pushed aside the assistant and hurried in to get the scoop.

"Welcome to the show, Marisela." She clasped my mother's hand in hers and adopted an expression of great concern. "What kind of lies, exactly, can't you live with?"

"Everything!" Mom rubbed her eyes with shaking hands. "My kids, my family . . . it's all a lie."

Remy leaned in. "How so?"

My mom's tears had been replaced by a flinty-eyed stridency. "I've made a lot of mistakes over the years. A lot. But this . . . I can't do this. I can't ask my children to cover for me."

"But we want to cover for you." Thomas sounded desperate.

"Yeah," I said. "We're *begging* to cover for you."

"No, no, keep going." Remy's hand adjusted the mic clipped to her crisp green blouse, and I realized that she might be recording this whole conversation. "Tell me, Marisela, what kinds of mistakes have you made?"

"I'm a horrible mother." My mom's voice was calm and firm. "I haven't been there when they needed me. I've run away from my responsibilities. I've kept my children a secret all these years, and by God, I'm not going to make them go on national television and lie about what a good mother I am."

I stared helplessly down at the notes I'd made with Ashley. This was definitely not in the script.

"Go home, kids." My mom rushed over to the door and held it open. "Get while the getting's good."

"But . . ." Thomas's mouth was hanging open.

"I'm sorry I ever asked you to do this. I know you don't believe I want to be a real mom, but I do. I'm going to prove that to you."

"So you have something to prove to your children?" Remy asked, her gaze sharp.

"Absolutely." Mom sniffled.

"Can we talk about it on-air?"

"If we must. But Eva and Thomas aren't doing this interview." Mom motioned us toward the door like we were dodging sniper fire. "Go on, you two. You can leave."

Thomas seemed torn for a moment, then decided to take her at her word. He raced out toward the parking lot and didn't look back.

"Eva?" My mother looked dignified, almost stately.

I stole a glance at Remy, who couldn't believe her luck. She was all but rubbing her hands together and cackling. "I'm not leaving you here all alone."

"That's sweet, baby girl, but I'll be fine."

"No, you won't." I glared at Remy. "And Ashley's going to have a heart attack."

"I can handle Ashley," Mom said. "And I can handle this interview. Now scoot. Who's the parent here, you or me?"

I furrowed my brow. "Is this a trick question?"

"I'm not going to ask you again. Go home. I'll call you tonight and tell you how it went. Here." She dug a twenty dollar bill out of her pocket. "Go get some ice cream with your brother." Then she turned to Remy. "Give me two minutes to touch up my eyes and we'll film. It's time I finally told the truth."

As I followed Thomas out to the parking lot, money in hand, I had to laugh. For the first time in eighteen years, my mother sounded, well, almost maternal.

# 15

Power agent Laurel Cordes is famous for her ruthless negotiation style, but my sources whisper that "the Tiger Shark" may not be completely heartless after all. Seems Ms. Cordes forgot the cardinal rule of agenting—never get involved with your clients—and fell hard for a certain blond hardbody in her stable. The much-younger man must have wearied of playing the brainless boy toy; after he scored his first big role, he ditched the elder

Miss C. and jumped ship to TNP. There's no relief in sight for Laurel, as her family life's even messier than her love life. Little sister Marisela just taped a three-hanky tell-all with Remy Johansen. Word from the set is that Mari's gone from label whore to attention whore. Ouch!

"'The elder Miss C.'?" I read the G-Spot item into the speaker of my fancy new phone as I got out of the Goose at the UCLA parking garage. "Somewhere, Laurel is having a stroke."

"Was she really serious about that guy?" Teague asked on the other end of the line. "He didn't seem to have much to him, other than muscles and hair."

I couldn't answer that question without feeling like I was betraying Laurel's confidence, so I just said, "Forget the part about Gavin—they called my aunt old! And my mom an attention whore! Heads will roll."

He paused for a moment. "You didn't tell me your mother was doing an interview with Remy Johansen."

I pushed down the lock on the driver's side door with my thumb—no fancy, automatic locking system in the Goose—and shrugged. "The less talking I do about that, the happier I'll be." I changed the subject as I followed the thick concrete walls toward the elevator. "This parking structure is like a bunker from World War Two or something. I can't believe this phone hasn't dropped the call yet. I guess that's the miracle of the Filament."

"The miracle of the swag bag." He laughed.

"I still can't believe you just gave this away. My roommates are totally jealous. Even my aunt wanted to know where I got it. She says she's still on the wait list for one."

"Tell her I'll try to score her one backstage at the MTV Movie Awards."

"You get to go to that? Lucky."

"I'm presenting." Another pause. "Do you want to go?"

"With you?" I frowned. "Like a date?"

"Such enthusiasm," he deadpanned. "Don't hurt yourself."

"No, of course I'll go with you. It's just, I thought . . . I don't know. We're done filming at the end of the week, and then you're going back to New York."

"I don't want to talk about this over the phone," he said. "When are you going to be on-set?"

"About three minutes." I exited the parking garage and crossed the street near the library.

"Good. And remember, keep your weekend free."

"Where are we going?" I asked for the zillionth time.

"You have to tell me! The suspense is keeping me awake at night."

"Beg all you want, baby—I'll never tell." He clicked off the line.

I was still smiling when I saw Danny waiting for me outside the perimeter of the set. He was back in his usual uniform of jeans, sweatshirt, and baseball cap, and the security guys were keeping an eye on him but hadn't asked him to move along.

"Hey." My smile faded as I tucked the tiny silver phone into my bag. "What are you doing here?"

"I figured you might be filming today." His eyes were shaded by his cap and I couldn't decipher his expression. "My stepmother mentioned you got a part on *Westchester County,* and—"

"Nina talks about me?" Danny's stepmother—aka C Money's mom—was a very powerful casting agent, and she and I hadn't gotten off to the best start.

"C Money asked her about you at brunch over the weekend. You know Nina—always got her ear to the ground."

"C Money." I shook my head. "He's persistent, I'll give him that. Listen, I know you're probably here to talk about what happened at Claude on Saturday."

"Yeah, how's Jacinda doing?"

I paused. "Jacinda?"

He nodded. "She seemed pretty upset when I left."

"She's okay, I think." I'd tried to sit her down for a heart-to-heart, but she was having none of it. "She always bounces back—she's starting this crazy new health kick."

"Good." He didn't seem inclined to say anything else.

"Is that why you're here?" I tried to keep the disappointment out of my tone. "To check on Jacinda?"

He shoved both hands into his jeans pockets. "Not entirely."

"Oh." I glanced at the behemoth security guards not twenty feet away. "I wish we could go sit down somewhere, but I have to be in hair and makeup in ten minutes—"

"That's okay." He seemed relieved. Hmph. "I just wanted to finish what I started to say out in the alley."

"Right. When I said I was sorry and you said you knew and then you maybe we could, dot, dot, dot." Not that I'd memorized our whole conversation and replayed it multiple times in my head. Nooo.

He gave me a look. " 'Dot, dot, dot'?"

"Well, you never finished your big proclamation." I'd finished it a hundred ways in my head, though. I was so afraid to hope that he missed me, but . . . what if he did? What if he finally realized that I hadn't meant to hurt him?

"Wait," I said, raising my fingers until I almost touched his lips. "Hang on. Before you say anything else, there's something I have to tell you. I don't want to keep secrets from you anymore—I learned my lesson on that."

He tilted his head, urging me to continue.

"I'm kind of dating again."

I didn't expect him to start ranting and raving, but I thought he might at least flinch. *Something*. He didn't move a muscle, though, so I took a deep breath and kept going.

"I don't want you to think I'm trying to hide that from you."

He blinked. Twice. "Oh."

"It's not serious, though. Just a fling. Just fun." Just a way to get over you. "So if you . . . I mean, if we . . ." I threw up my hands. "Okay, you talk now. I'll shut up."

I clamped my lips together and waited.

He lifted the brim of his baseball cap several times, as if signaling to a catcher behind home plate. "I know you're seeing someone. Teague Archer, right?"

"Yeah, how did you—"

"I read that thing in the G-Spot and figured it was you," he said. "You're moving on. We both are."

Did he have to sound so content about that?

"When we broke up, I never wanted to see you again.

I didn't think I could ever be around you without think-ing about—"

"I know," I keened. "I know."

"But now, I guess . . ." He shoved the hat back down on his forehead. "We still like each other, right? We can still talk."

"Definitely."

"That's what I was going to say on Saturday night. Maybe we can be friends now. If you want."

I swallowed back my disappointment. "Sounds good."

He smiled then, a real smile. "So we'll start fresh."

"Yeah. I . . . have to go." I pivoted toward the set and called over my shoulder, "I guess I'll see you around."

"Okay." He waved. "I'll call you."

I rushed past the phalanx of security and into the safe seclusion of *Westchester County.* Teague was waiting for me outside his trailer.

"What a guy." I went up on tiptoe and kissed him on the lips.

"Hey." He wrapped his arms around me. "What was that for?"

"Nothing," I murmured. "Just for being you."

"Glad to be of service. But who else would I be?"

I held him tighter and didn't answer.

# 16

"Popcorn?" Thomas passed me the red-and-white bag of microwaved, slightly burnt kettle corn.

"Ugh." I waved the bag away. "No. I'm too nervous to eat."

"Don't worry. I'm sure it'll be fine." But he couldn't look away from the TV screen, either.

I fidgeted. "How much longer?"

"Seven minutes."

Thomas had come over to the apartment in West Hollywood to watch the official Marisela Cordes tell-all interview debut on network television. We camped out on the sofa with sodas and snacks, trying to pretend we weren't nervous wrecks.

"Has she called you since they taped on Monday?" he asked.

I shook my head. "Nope. You?"

"Uh-uh."

"Well, this should be interesting."

"Yeah." He shoved some popcorn in his mouth. "Life used to be so boring before Marisela showed up."

"Welcome to my world."

We stared at the commercials flashing across the muted screen. I gave up fidgeting and started gnawing my lower lip. Thomas jiggled his foot against the coffee table.

"I like what you've done with the place," he said, gesturing to the assortment of fashion magazines, empty Red Bull cans, and inside-out athletic wear strewn all over the carpet. "Very frat house."

"Don't blame me for the mess. Blame—"

A key rattled in the lock, then Jacinda strutted in from the courtyard.

"There she is," I said as she breezed in, sweating in

tiny white shorts and a tinier blue sports bra. "Did you go running again?"

"Four miles. I'm thinking about training for a marathon." She dropped her keys on the small table next to the door, then braced her hands against the doorframe and lunged back to stretch her calf.

I laughed—I couldn't help myself. *"You're* going to train for a marathon?"

"Why is that funny?" She leaned over to touch her toes. "You're just jealous because now I'm going to look hotter than ever. Plus, I'll be able to outrun everyone else at the sample sales on Rodeo."

I glanced at the TV. Still commercials. "Whatever keeps you motivated."

"The only problem is, these long runs get hella boring all by myself, and Coelle's shooting schedule is crazy, so she always wants to get up and work out at like five A.M. What a masochist. Do you want to train with me?"

"Hmm . . ." I thought it over for one and a half seconds. "Nope."

"I'll run with you," Thomas volunteered.

"What? Since when do you run?" I asked. That's when I noticed his face. His eyes went glassy and his jaw went slack as he stared at my beautiful blonde roommate in her skimpy little outfit. "Thomas? Hello? Earth to Thomas!"

His eyes snapped back into focus. "I was on the cross-country team in high school. I've been looking for a running buddy."

Jacinda stopped stretching and gave him a flirty eyelash flutter. Her long hair was tied back in a ponytail, but that didn't stop her from flipping it. "You must be Eva's brother, right?"

"Yeah." He shot into a standing position and almost tripped over his own feet in his haste to shake her hand. "Thomas. Nice to meet you."

"Jacinda Crane-Laird." Ignoring my glower, she slipped her fingers into his and held on way longer than necessary. "You're a runner?"

Thomas nodded eagerly.

"Well." She gave him a frank once-over. "You don't look like a runner. You have a swimmer's build—and that's a good thing."

"Excuse me," I huffed. "Jacinda, may I have a word with you?"

She ignored me and kept checking out at my brother's pecs. "I'm just starting to train, so I probably can't keep up with someone as tall and strong as you, but if you're willing to go easy on me . . ."

"Jacinda!" I yelled. *"Now!"*

"Where are your manners? Can't you see I'm meeting your brother?"

I got up, yanked her out into the courtyard, and shut the door behind us.

"Well?" She planted her hands on her hips. "What's your problem?"

"He's my *brother.*" I jabbed my thumb back toward the door. "That means hands off."

"I'm not doing anything!" she protested. "He's the one who offered to go running with me!"

"Yeah, because you're hooching around in your little Spandex shorts and flashing your abs all over the place! Jeez, girl, don't you ever put on a shirt?"

"Shirts screw up my tan lines!" she fired back. "And I'm not doing anything wrong."

"You're hitting on my brother!"

"Wrong—I'm letting him hit on me. Very important distinction."

"Well, *don't* let him. He's off-limits to you."

"Give me one good reason why."

"Because you're totally evil and you're going to break his heart?"

She grinned. "Oh, come on, I'm not totally evil. I'm only, like, ninety-two percent evil."

Thomas started to open the door, but I kicked it shut with the back of my heel. "Leave him alone, I mean it."

She lifted her chin. "Make me."

"Do not do this," I warned her. "There are five million other guys in this city. You don't need Thomas."

She dropped the haughty routine and tried to look vulnerable and sensitive. "But he seems so nice. Maybe I'm ready to date a nice guy, for a change."

"Maybe," I allowed. "But could you please test that theory with someone else?"

"You don't think I'm good enough for your precious brother?"

"Don't make this into—"

Thomas pushed the door open again. "What's going on out here?"

"Nothing," I said quickly.

Jacinda, who had apparently attended the same advanced-level classes in male manipulation that my mother had, let her eyes tear up. She clasped her hands behind her back (the better to showcase her cleavage) and murmured, "Eva doesn't think it's a good idea for us to go running together."

"Why not?" Thomas demanded. He looked shocked and betrayed and utterly entranced with the Spandex shorts.

"Because," I ground out, "you've got so much going on with classes and your band that, uh—"

Jacinda's eyes lit up. "Ooh, you're in a band?"

Crap.

"Yeah, I play bass," Thomas said. "We're not the next Green Day or anything, but we play bars up in the Valley occasionally."

"Really?" She went all gushy and gooey. "I'd love to come to see you play sometime."

"You're too cool for the Valley," I reminded her, but it was too late. They were cooing at each other like punch-drunk pigeons on a window ledge.

I cleared my throat. "So anyway, we better get inside. Mom's interview is starting."

"Right." Thomas finally closed his mouth. "We should watch."

Jacinda winked at me over his shoulder. "You guys go ahead. I'm going to rinse off and slip into something a little more comfortable." She smiled triumphantly and escaped upstairs.

"Okay." I returned to the threadbare lavender couch and unmuted the television. "Here we go."

Thomas plunked down next to me, but he kept stealing glances toward the stairs.

Remy Johansen's flawless face appeared in a close-up

as she introduced her subject. "Marisela Cordes doesn't believe in doing anything halfway. From her heyday as a cover girl in the eighties to her struggle with addiction in the nineties, she's always pushed her limits. Before we introduce a new generation to one of fashion's most controversial, charismatic faces, let's take a look at how this small-town girl from the Berkshires made her mark in Hollywood . . ."

While they cut to a photo montage of my mom's early modeling shoots, I tried to reason with my brother. "So now you've met Jacinda."

He nodded. "She's really something."

"Yeah, about that . . . I know she's beautiful, but I've seen Jacinda go through a lot of guys, and trust me, you don't want to get involved with her."

"Eva!"

"I saw the way you were looking at her."

"Well, of course I was looking at her!" He reddened. "She should be on the cover of *Maxim*. But that doesn't mean I want to, quote, get involved with her."

I raised my eyebrows. "Really."

"She's hot, no doubt, but not my type. So don't worry."

I checked the TV, where the modeling retrospective

had moved on to a rundown of my mother's rock star paramours. "Okay. I just don't want you to get, you know, your feelings hurt."

"This from the girl who's dating Teague Archer?" he said.

I feigned bewilderement. "What are you—"

"Come on, I heard all about it. And don't worry—I can take care of myself."

"And I can take care of myself."

"Then I guess we don't have any problems."

"I guess not."

"Good."

"Good."

"Fine."

Before Remy Johansen wrapped up her recap of my mother's biography, Jacinda made her grand entrance in a clingy black skirt, a tight strapless white top, and enough perfume to fumigate the entire apartment complex.

"So?" she purred. "How's the interview?"

"Great," I said. "You going out? Have a nice time. *Bye.*"

"I'm positively famished after that run." She drifted over to Thomas's side of the couch. "But you guys have probably already had dinner."

"I haven't," my brother said, even though he'd gone through a bag of popcorn and half a cold pizza in the last two hours.

She produced a bottle of moisturizer and slathered lotion on her bare legs. "There's a new sushi place in Los Feliz I've been dying to try, but I don't want to go alone."

"Let's go." The boy who just minutes ago had claimed Jacinda wasn't his type vaulted over the back of the couch.

"Hey!" I cried. "What about the interview?"

"Can you record it?" He grabbed his car keys. "Thanks."

Jacinda eyed the keys. "What do you drive?"

Thomas looked deeply ashamed. "A Honda."

She pulled her keys out of her purse and dangled them in his face. "I've got a Benz. You want to drive it?"

Ten seconds later, they were gone and I was left alone with the trainwreck unfolding on the TV screen.

"Tell me about your son and daughter," Remy urged. "Is it true you've been estranged from them over the years?"

"I got pregnant at a very young age and the truth is, I haven't always been there for my kids." My mother, looking stunning, paused for a shaky sigh and a single perfectly timed tear. "I've let them down. I've been too afraid to get attached. But now that I'm older and wiser, I'd like to try parenthood again. I'm hoping to have another baby this year."

# 17

I showed up at my aunt's doorstep the next day with a tub of fudge ripple ice cream and a foil-covered plate of brownies. Her BMW was in the driveway, so I knew she was home.

"Evie," she said when she came to the door in tailored gray pants and a black cashmere sweater. "What are you doing here? Are we—did I schedule a dinner with you and forget?"

"No." I offered up the fat-laden goodies. "But I was

hoping we could do a postmortem on Mom's interview."

She frowned. "You brought me eighty thousand calories' worth of butterfat and chocolate for that?"

I squirmed under her piercing gaze. "Well, and I thought you might be feeling a little . . . you know. After the whole thing with Gavin."

"I see." She stared at the ice cream like the label was written in Sanskrit, and I realized my mistake. Brownies from a mix and store-bought ice cream were the kind of thing *I* ate when *I* was depressed. Aunt Laurel probably preferred imported Belgian truffles and Camembert cheese smeared on a French baguette. "Well, that's very thoughtful of you, but I don't need cheering up."

"Oh, give it up," said a familiar voice from the foyer. "You're miserable and we all know it."

"Mom?" I peered over my aunt's shoulder.

"Hi, baby girl." My mom, wearing long, slim jeans and a complicated strappy red top, opened her arms for a hug. Rhett the death poodle was right behind her, yapping up a storm. "How'd you like the interview? Was my makeup job kick-ass or what?"

"Are you serious about trying to have another baby?" I babbled. "This year? Right now? Because I really think—"

My mom exchanged a look with my aunt and they both burst out laughing. "Oh, darling, of course

I'm not going to have another baby. Don't you know that you can't believe anything a celebrity tells the media?"

"Then why—"

"Controversy, Evie. I'm making my big comeback and I need to get people talking. Ashley called me this morning and said that I'm going to be featured in two of the big weekly magazines next week. Score!"

I turned to Laurel, who just rolled her eyes and ushered me into the house. "But aren't you worried that people will say you're an unfit parent?" I pressed.

"Are you kidding?" Mom crowed. "I hope they *do!* Then I can cry sexism and say if I were a man, no one would think twice about my starting a second family at forty. Then, next thing you know, I'm doing the talk show circuit—maybe even *Oprah*. She loves a good redemption story."

"So you want everyone to rip on your mothering skills, but you don't actually want to be a mother," I clarified.

"Well, I won't have time for a baby." She kissed my cheek. "Imagine what pregnancy would do to my figure at this stage of the game. And the sleep deprivation and the morning sickness . . . ugh. Anyway, where would I find the time? Between my new TV show and the press junket and my book deal—"

My jaw dropped. "What book deal?"

"*Fashion Statements: Lessons in Life and Love from a Crazy Cover Girl* by Marisela Cordes," Aunt Laurel announced with a mercenary smile. "I'm putting the proposal together this weekend, and we're going to start the bidding war in New York at half a mil."

"Shut up! How are you going to write a book? You won't even answer your e-mail!" I pointed out.

"Well, I don't have to worry about grammar and spelling and all that annoying stuff," Mom said. "I'm the idea woman! I'll tell all my outrageous stories and share my personal philosophy and my coauthor will take care of the mundane details."

"You're hiring a ghost writer?"

"Coauthor," Mom corrected. "Dr. Naomi Hutch. She's a psychologist in Malibu. Very insightful. My therapist recommended her."

"Together, Mari and Dr. Hutch make the perfect team—juicy Hollywood experience meets clinical expertise." My aunt practically had cartoon dollar signs where her pupils should be. "Very commercial, very marketable."

"I'm going to be a mentor and a role model," my mom informed me. "And I'm going to make a ton of money doing it. Are you proud of me?"

"Hey, as long as you're not having another kid, I'll be

whatever you want me to be," I said. "And when did you start seeing a therapist?"

"Last month." Mom looked sheepish. "Laurel said she'd kick me out of the guesthouse if I didn't."

Interesting. That might explain the sudden crisis of conscience in Remy Johansen's greenroom. "So how's that going?" I asked.

"Fine, I guess." Big, gusty sigh. "We have to spend all our time talking about *feelings*. She keeps telling me to stop focusing on my outside and start focusing on the inside, which is a waste, considering how much time and effort I put into looking hot. I mean, honestly, I didn't get a boob job and an eye lift so I could spend all day yapping about my childhood. Everyone thinks it's so easy being a supermodel, but I am here to tell you that it is not!"

"Uh-huh." I managed to keep a straight face. "Is that what you're going to say in your book?"

"Yes, and I'm also going to warn my readers not to date guys who want you to dress up like Cat Woman every time you sleep with them. I learned that one the hard way."

My aunt scooped up Rhett, who was gnawing on the bottom stair tread. "I'll put the ice cream in the freezer and open a bottle of wine. Mari, do you want a glass?"

"Always."

"Eva?"

"Sure." I tried to sound casual and blasé.

But my mother shook her head. "Laurel, she can't have wine, she's underage."

My aunt and I both gaped at her.

"Well, she is," Mom insisted.

"You let me drink champagne out of the bottle a few weeks ago," I reminded her.

"Oh right." She looked disappointed. "I forgot about that."

"And before that, you wanted to buy me my first mimosa. Don't you think it's a little late to be playing the 'you're underage' card?"

"My therapist says I need to set boundaries with you. I'm your mother and you have to listen to me."

"Relax, Mari, it's one glass and we'll be sitting right here with her. I've got a nice bottle of cabernet and it's time she starts to develop a more sophisticated palate."

Yep. Laurel had definitely been horrified by my choice of brownies and ice cream.

"Okay, fine, but no drinking and driving." Mom wagged her index finger at me.

"Oh my God. Who *are* you?"

"What?" Mom shrugged. "Isn't that what moms do? Yell at you and tell you not to drink and drive?"

Now that she mentioned it, that was pretty much what my friends' mothers did. Of course, my friends' moms also stuck around to raise them and didn't keep their father's and/or brothers' identities secret for eighteen years. But, for the first time in forever, she was actually trying. So I decided to try, too. "Yeah. Good job."

She perked up. "So I sound like a real mom?"

"Sure. All you need now is some cupcakes and a minivan."

"Did you hear that, Laurel? I'm an honorary soccer mom!"

"I'll drink to that." My aunt came back out of the kitchen carrying three long-stemmed goblets filled with deep red wine. The three of us sat down on the pristine white sofa in the living room and my aunt ignited the gas fireplace with a touch of a remote-control button.

Laurel raised her wineglass to her nose and inhaled deeply. "Mmm. Nice bouquet. Black currant with a hint of cedar. Can you smell it, pet?"

I stuck my nose down my glass and sniffed. The wine smelled like, well, wine. But I nodded knowingly and said, "Absolutely."

"A good cabernet will always have a currant overtone. If it doesn't, that means the grapes were harvested too early or the soil was too rich."

"Uh-huh." Should I be writing this down?

My mother wasn't even pretending to listen. She took a giant swig, then another, then tugged at her bra strap under her shirt. Classy.

"Go ahead, Evie, taste it," Laurel urged.

Given the build-up with the currants and all, I was expecting it to taste delicious and fruity. Or at least cedar-y. But it tasted nasty and acidic. It took all my self-control not to spit it right back into the glass. "Yum," I choked out.

"See? A fine wine like this soothes the soul." My aunt relaxed and watched the flames leap in the fake fire. "Forget chocolate. All you need to get over a breakup is good wine, good company, and good jewelry."

That's when I noticed the massive diamond ring sparkling on her right hand. "Wow. Is that new?"

"Picked it out yesterday." Laurel held up her fingers so the diamond's facets sparkled in the sunlight. "I may not have a fiancé, but I can still have the rock."

"Ooh." My mom's eyes widened. "Can I borrow it?"

"Over my dead body."

Now I felt even worse about what had happened with Gavin during the kissing scene. "I didn't know you guys had talked about getting married."

"Oh, we hadn't," Laurel said. "He was way too young for me and besides, I'm not the marrying type."

"Plus, he was a selfish, sociopathic ass," my mom added.

Laurel sipped her wine. "I didn't like him that much anyway."

We all knew this was a lie, but no one contradicted her.

"I should put that in my book," my mom said. "Don't be afraid to buy your own bling."

"No one says 'bling' anymore, Mom," I informed her.

"But it's still a good lesson," Laurel said. "Are you listening, Evie? You can't put your life on hold, waiting for the perfect guy to come along at the perfect time. Sometimes you just have to seize the moment and do what makes you happy and to hell with the consequences."

# 18

"You have a passport, right?" Teague asked on Friday afternoon when we finished shooting our last scene together for *Westchester County*.

"Yeah." Although the only foreign stamp adorning its pages was a single Canadian seal from a debate club trip to Toronto last year. "Why?"

"Good." He started toward his trailer.

"Not so fast." I hooked my finger through the belt loop on his jeans. "You can't just casually ask me if

I have a passport and then go moseying off into the sunset."

He gave me that mildly amused (and majorly sexy) grin. "Patience isn't your strong suit, is it?"

"Nope." I ran my hands up along his arms. "Now where're we going? Mexico, right?"

For a second, he looked like his resolve was faltering, but then he shook his head and said, "No more details."

I grinned and whispered, "I have ways of making you talk."

"And I have ways of making you stop asking questions." He turned around, dipped me down the way he had when we first met in his trailer, and kissed me until I could barely remember my name, let alone my interrogation strategies. Then he set me back on my feet and announced, "I'll pick you up at eight sharp—bring your passport and comfortable shoes."

"What should I pack?" I called after him.

"Nothing."

"Not even a toothbrush?"

"Would Bella Santorini pack a toothbrush?"

Teague showed up right on time with black sunglasses, a battered black leather jacket, and a chauffered black Town Car idling at the curb. Jacinda wasn't home (probably off "running" with my brother—the horror, the horror), but I introduced Teague to Coelle, who, incredibly, seemed a little starstruck. She kept touching his arm and giggling. I'd never seen Coelle Banerjee giggle. Who knew she was even physically capable of it?

But that was the effect that Teague had on girls. He made them do things they'd never ordinarily do.

After Coelle finished gushing about how much she'd loved him in his last film role and how she never missed an episode of *Westchester County* (a shameless lie), Teague looked at me expectantly. "Ready?"

I pulled my passport out of my purse. "Ready."

"Where are you guys going?" Coelle asked, clearly dying to be invited along.

"Ask him," I said. "I'm on a need-to-know basis, apparently."

"That's right. And you don't need to know." Teague tucked my passport into his jacket pocket.

"When are you going to be back?" Coelle wanted to know.

I glanced at Teague. "I'll be back when I get back."

My roommate laughed. "Look at Little Miss Laissez-Faire. What have you done with the real Eva Cordes?"

"That seems to be the question of the day." I followed Teague out to the car and relaxed against the cool leather seats. The driver headed down La Cienega Boulevard for what seemed like hours and just when I started to settle in for the long drive to Mexico, we turned right and headed toward LAX.

"We're going to the airport!" I started bouncing around in my seat. "We're going to the airport!"

As the car wound around the many departures terminals, I started taking wild guesses about where we were headed: "Bermuda? Timbuktu? Iowa?"

"Why on earth would I take you to Iowa?" Teague asked.

"Aha! So you're *not* taking me to Iowa?"

"What did I say about questions like that?"

"Okay, so Iowa's out." I pretended to make notes on an invisible steno pad. "What about North Dakota?"

"I don't think we'd need passports to go to North Dakota."

"True. Okay . . . what about Jamaica?"

"Eva . . ."

"Costa Rica?" I glanced down at my jeans and thin blue sweater. "I hope it's someplace warm," I mused. "Ooh, are we going to Australia?"

"Not this time." He shook his head. "Now knock it off. You're not getting anything else out of me."

*Not this time.* Those words shut me up for a few minutes. "Not this time" implied that there would be a next time, which implied . . .

*Stop fixating on the future. Live in the moment for a change.*

I continued to speculate about our destination as we shuffled through the security line ("Tokyo?" "Stockholm?") and stopped at the food court ("Finland?" "Laos?") to buy muffins and sign autographs. Well, one of us signed autographs. I just waited on the sidelines and watched Teague turn on a completely charming and totally insincere smile for a hyperventilating flock of preadolescent girls.

Finally he handed me a boarding pass as we approached a British Airways gate. I scanned the thin slip of paper, then gasped. "London? Are you kidding me?"

"I can neither admit nor deny anything at this point in time," he said in an official, press conference voice.

"When are we coming back?"

"Monday night."

I did a few calculations in my head. "Holy crap. We're going to England for thirty-six hours?"

"Give or take a few time zones."

"But what will I wear?" I regarded my shlubby outfit in dismay.

"Hey." He tilted my face up until I looked him in the eye. "Trust me."

"But what am I going to wear all weekend? I didn't bring any—"

"Do you trust me?"

My gaze flickered down to the ticket—first class(!!!)—then back to his face. "Yeah."

"Then relax. We're having fun, remember?"

By the time our plane landed in the UK, I was jet-lagged and absolutely stuffed with first-class goodies: fruit plates, pastries, and enough hot tea to float the British Navy. I'd drifted off to sleep under a light wool blanket, feeling surprisingly relaxed as I breathed in Teague's scent and listened to the muffled thrum of the engines.

When I woke up, my clothes were rumpled, my breath was stale, and my leg muscles had started to cramp. My excitement ebbed into a dazed exhaustion, and when we shuffled off the plane into the arrivals area at Heathrow, I buried my head into Teague's chest and pleaded, "Bed. Pillow. Dark. Now."

He stroked my hair back from my face. "Hang on. We're almost there."

"Almost where?" I moaned. "I'm filthy and tired and totally adventured out."

"We have to catch a connecting flight. It'll be quick, I promise—just an hour or two. We're going to Venice."

We arrived at the Marco Polo Airport in Venice around dinnertime on Saturday, and Teague arranged for a water taxi to take us to our hotel. I reminded myself to take in the scenery, the ornate architecture and the startling aqua color of the water in the canals, but it was all I could do to keep my eyes open.

"I see a minibar raid in our immediate future," Teague announced as we entered the palatial lobby of the Hotel Gritti Palace. The opulence was overwhelming at first—gold wall sconces and gilt-inlaid celings offset massive dark oil paintings that looked like they dated all the way back to the Renaissance.

"I see sleep," I said. "The minibar can wait."

"Fair enough; sleep it is. We can have breakfast tomorrow morning on the canal. Hell, we can have breakfast in bed."

"Yeah. Speaking of which . . ." I rubbed my eyes and tried to stay alert. "I know we're sharing a room and all, but I'm not, uh . . . I don't . . ."

He raised one eyebrow. "You're afraid I'll take advantage of your jet-lagged stupor?"

"Well . . ." I kind of *wanted* him to take advantage of my jet-lagged stupor, but no way could I say that out loud.

"Uh-huh." His grin was positively wicked. "Don't worry—I'll seduce you soon enough."

# 19

I woke up twelve hours later, nestled in the soft cotton robe that I'd found folded in the hotel bathroom. Teague was sprawled out next to me with his arm slung across my back, although the bed was so big that we could have both made snow angels in the pristine white sheets without touching each other. As it turned out, I hadn't needed to worry about a toothbrush—the hotel had been happy to provide one, along with all the miniature soaps, lotions, and shampoos a girl could ever want.

"Hey." I nudged Teague's ankle with my foot. "You awake?"

"Mmph." He was sleeping in a pair of blue boxers with his chest bare. His jaw sported a dark stubble and he looked like he should be in a travel brochure somewhere. Or a cologne ad. Or a steamy romance novel.

This perfect, handsome, unpredictable guy was in *my* bed in the most romantic city in the world. Not for the first time, it occurred to me that I should really do something besides ogle his abs and prod his ankle.

So I slid my foot higher up his leg and kissed him. "This is your wake-up call."

He opened one eye. "I'm intrigued. What do I get if I hit the snooze button?"

"Girls don't have snooze buttons," I informed him. "It's now or never."

"Okay, then now." He rolled over and started working on the knot in my robe belt.

"Not so fast." I wriggled out from under him and headed for the bathroom. "We're in Venice; we're going to see Venice. I didn't come all this way to spend the whole day in bed."

"But it's such a nice bed," he coaxed, and I had to

agree with that. We had a huge, airy room with a view of the Grand Canal, heavy brocade curtains, and antique furniture. A delicate china vase full of fresh red roses sat atop a marble side table, and a crystal chandelier sparkled above the massive bed.

"I thought we were going to have an adventure?" I reminded him.

"We are. In bed."

"Don't worry," I teased, "I'll seduce you soon enough."

A hot shower was just what I needed after all those hours on the plane yesterday. I luxuriated in the steam and the sweet, floral scents of the shampoo. When I padded back into the bedroom, Teague had managed to procure a room service tray laden with fresh coffee and flaky pastries.

We ate breakfast by the window, mesmerized by the shimmering surface of the canal. The noise and rush and stress of Hollywood seemed light-years away. "I wonder who's stayed in this room before us," I mused.

"Kings, queens, celebrities," Teague said. "You fit right in."

"Yeah." I slouched back in my damp robe and wet hair. "Princess Eva. How many kings and queens do you think wore the same jeans and sweater for three days running?"

He smiled at me over the rim of his coffee cup. "Oh, you're not going to be wearing jeans and a sweater today."

"Well, I don't think this robe is going to cut it. I've heard the Italians are pretty fashion forward. So unless you feel like making something out of the curtains . . ."

"We're going shopping," he announced. "Piazza San Marco has some of the best shopping in Europe. And don't worry—your Italian wardrobe is on me."

"Teague, no!" I protested. "No way! You already paid for the flight—"

"Hey, this trip was my idea, and you deserve to celebrate filming your first TV role. Besides, I'm the one who told you not to pack anything."

"But this hotel must cost a fortune—"

"Exactly. You're staying in a palace, you need to dress accordingly."

I nibbled my pane e cioccalata. "But I feel so high-class hooker."

"Royalty," he corrected. "Not hooker. And if it'll make you feel better, you can buy me something, too."

"Like a Versace suit?"

"Like an espresso."

"Yeah, that sounds totally fair."

"I'm glad you agree."

\* \* \*

Piazza San Marco was like Rodeo Drive with subtitles. Teague took me to a boutique filled with opulent designer clothes and encouraged me to try on everything from plain white button-down shirts to sequined ballgowns. The sales staff recognized him immediately and fawned over both of us. I ended up with a simple blue wool dress, funky black pumps, and sunglasses that cost more than my laptop. Teague also insisted I buy an outfit for the trip home, so I chose a wickedly well-cut pair of jeans and a white blouse that made me look like I actually had curves. Then he insisted I had to get a new purse to go with the new dress. And a feather-light cashmere cardigan "in case you get cold."

"Stop," I pleaded. "You're spoiling me."

"So what?" he asked.

"So . . ." I glanced at the salesclerks, who were hanging on to our every word. "I'll never be able to go back to real life after this. You're going to ruin me for all other men, you know."

"My plan is working. Now stop freaking out and enjoy yourself. What are you so afraid of?"

For himself, he picked out jeans by an Italian designer I'd never heard of and a crisp pale blue shirt. We changed into our new apparel, sent the rest of the clothes back to the hotel, and set out to explore the city on foot.

For hours, we wandered the cobblestone streets, ducking into shops and galleries and trying to approach the stray cats that roamed the winding pathways. The local artisans were incredible—I spotted a gorgeous pair of sapphire earrings in a jeweler's window, but didn't dare mention them because I knew Teague would insist on adding them to my ever-growing pile of loot. We had lunch on a terrace overlooking the bay, then made our way to the Guggenheim Museum.

We lapsed into silence as we stopped to study Picassos, Chagalls, and Kandinskys. The quiet let me really study the paintings and feel some of the fear I'd been trying so hard to deny for the last few weeks. Fear that Thomas would decide he didn't feel like dealing with me and my mom anymore, fear that my mother would give up her sudden attempt to be close to me and go back to the way she'd always been, fear that I'd never love anyone else the way I'd loved Danny.

"What?" Teague finally asked when we stopped to soak up Magritte's *L'Empire des Lumieres*. "You look sad."

"I'm just thinking. You were right about what you said this morning—I'm tired of being afraid. It's definitely time I let myself live a little."

Then I took his hand and whispered, "Take me back to the hotel."

# 20

"You sure you're ready for this?" Teague asked as we tumbled onto the bed's red satin quilt.

I didn't answer, just kissed him and let my body sink into the cool, soft cushioning. The dark shadows in the corners of the room swallowed up the pink glow of the setting sun. I couldn't shake the surreal sense that this was all a dream, a fantasy.

Teague was still holding back. "But you said—"

"Shhh." I reached up to run my fingers along his cheek. "Don't ruin it."

I sat up and twisted around to wrestle with the zipper on my dress. Teague drew back for a moment, studying the expression on my face.

"But what about—"

"Stop talking," I pleaded, almost desperate.

So he did. He shut up and finished unzipping my dress. My heart felt like it was ricocheting around my ribcage.

"Eva." He brushed my hair aside and pressed his lips against the base of my neck. "Calm down. There's no rush."

I couldn't stifle a nervous burst of laughter. "I know. I'm just . . ."

"I know." His hands kneaded the tension out of my shoulders. I closed my eyes and stretched out on my stomach, trying to focus on the sensations washing over me. The feel of his skin against mine. The slow, tender confidence in his touch.

As he started to kiss his way down my spine, I started to feel buzzed and tingly and I hadn't even taken my dress all the way off. I tucked my face into a pillow and promised myself that no matter what happened after tonight, I'd never regret this. I was awake and alive in a whole new way.

"You all right?" he murmured.

I suppressed a little shiver and nodded. Then, slowly, I stood up and let the dress drop to the floor. I faced him in the fading light, nearly naked and completely vulnerable, and let him look at me. I wasn't afraid or ashamed.

As the first sprinkling of stars started shining in the foreign night sky, we embarked on our biggest adventure yet.

*Sex changes everything.* Aunt Laurel had given me that warning in one of her incredibly awkward pseudo-maternal lectures. "Sex clouds your judgment, but at the same time, it intensifies your emotions," she'd said. "Whatever you feel about someone, once you have sex with them, you'll feel that to the tenth power. So be careful who you sleep with."

At the time, I'd had no way of knowing if she was telling the truth or just trying to scare me into joining a convent.

But I realized that there was a possibility sex would make me fall in love with Teague. If I let my guard down for a second, I'd be head over heels. He was smart and sweet and fun and good for me in a weird, unexpected way.

Plus, he was . . . well, Jacinda always said I would know right away if a guy was good in bed, and Teague definitely was. I didn't need a lot of experience to know that. It wasn't so much what he did; it was how he made me feel: fascinating and beautiful and totally adored. Like I was the only woman in the world.

After he drifted off to sleep, I wrapped myself up in the plush terry cloth robe, walked over to the window, and stared out into the starry sky for hours. I'd never felt less like sleeping in my life.

*Bzz, bzz, bzz.* My Filament vibrated on the small marble table near the bed. It was the one item I'd brought from home, in addition to my keys, my purse, and the clothes on my back.

I snatched up the sleek silver gadget before it woke Teague. The illuminated screen revealed a short text message from Danny Bristow:

Saturday night-R U out and about?

For a second, I thought I might literally have a heart attack. I clapped one hand to my chest and glanced guiltily across the hotel room, as if Danny could peer through the wireless connection and see my dishevelment, my lips still swollen from too much kissing.

With shaking fingers I texted back:

No. Staying in. U?

"Thanks so much for everything." I accepted the blanket he offered. "This trip, the dive bar in Malibu, that kiss when we first met . . ."

He laughed. "The look on your face. I thought you were going to murder me on the spot."

"I considered it," I said loftily.

"Thanks for letting me live." He turned off his phone and crammed it into one of the shopping bags that doubled as our carry-on luggage. "We've had a good time." He gave me a look, and I knew he was thinking about last night. "A *very* good time."

"Yeah." I stared out the window and tried to ignore the little pricks of guilt. *Miss you, too.*

"Hey." He waited until I turned back to him. "We should keep doing this."

"What? Going to Europe? Buying criminally expensive clothes?"

"No, I mean this." He had stopped smiling. "You and me."

I froze. "You mean like a relationship?"

"Yeah." His blue eyes darkened. "Let's give it a shot. For real."

"I thought you had all these rules about 'just fun, no strings'?"

"Screw that." He lowered his voice as the flight attendant passed by to do her final passenger check before takeoff. "Let's have strings, what the hell."

"You're serious?"

"Dead right."

"But . . ." My mind whirled. This was what I'd been secretly hoping for ever since I first met him at the casting audition. He was my dream man! So why wasn't I a blathering, blissed-out mess? "But how? I've never dated long distance before."

"Forget the long-distance thing—that never lasts." He took my hand as the plane started taxiing down the runway. "Come to New York with me."

His enthusiasm was contagious. "Okay!" I grinned. "I don't have any jobs booked in the next few weeks, so—"

"No, I mean you can *move* to New York."

"Oh." I paused. "As in live there? Permanently?"

"Right." He unleashed the full force of the Teague Archer charm on me.

The plane took off and started climbing toward the clouds. He had to raise his voice to make himself heard over the roar of the engines. "You could move into my apartment in Manhattan and start working out there. I'm sure my agent would sign you—"

"Whoa." I held up a hand. "I am not firing Laurel. Besides the fact that she's family, she'd hunt me down like a dog. I'm too young to die."

"Then you can arrange something with one of her East Coast affiliates. Whatever. And then, when I have to do films on location, you can go with me."

I sat back for a minute, trying to process all this. "So I'd actually *move* to New York. I'd give up the apartment in West Hollywood and move in with you?"

"Right. If you want. If you'd rather have your own apartment, we could arrange for that, too. So don't worry."

"I'm not worried." I paused. "I'm just a little overwhelmed. I mean, moving across the country—"

"You moved across the country to come to Los Angeles, didn't you?" he pressed.

"Sort of." I'd actually moved across the country to track down my mom. Los Angeles had been incidental. If she'd lived in Orlando, I'd probably be narrating the Jungle Cruise at Disney World right now.

"So what's one more move? You can come with me to sets in Toronto and New Zealand—we'll go all over the world together. My *Westchester County* contract's up at the end of the season, and my agent keeps talking about making the jump to features full-time."

I lost myself in the fantasy of globe-trotting with Teague. It would be like Venice every day. Except better, because he wasn't Teague Archer the celebrity to me anymore. He was just Teague. The real person had turned out to be even better than the public persona.

This surreal, untouchable feeling never had to end.

But it would cost me everything I'd found in L.A.

"So being your girlfriend would kind of be my job?" I clarified.

"No!" he insisted. "God, no. You would have your own career, your own life."

"But how?" I kept my tone light. "If I were traveling with you all over the world? You said it yourself—your life isn't normal. Who would I be if I went with you?"

He pulled away. "You don't want to go to New York."

"Yes, I do." I leaned in to close the distance he'd put between us. "But I don't have a normal life, either; that's why I came to L.A. in the first place. I've just started to get to know my brother, and my mom and I are finally starting to—well, I don't know exactly what we're starting to do, but we're finally making progress. I've been waiting for that since I was in preschool. Plus, it's hard because . . ." My cheeks felt like they were going up in flames. "Can I tell you the truth? I kind of . . . I feel like I could fall in love with you."

"I know," he said matter-of-factly.

"You are so arrogant." I rolled my eyes.

"I'm confident. There's a difference."

I couldn't resist. "Oh really? What's the difference?"

He shrugged. "I have the goods to back it up."

"*God,* you're arrogant!" We both laughed.

"But you love it. So come with me to New York."

I exhaled slowly. "I feel like you're asking me to choose between being myself and being your girlfriend. And remember what you said about Hollywood being a game?"

"Yeah."

"Well, you know what happens to you when the game is over. You're going to go back to Australia and live on a ranch and go for walkabouts in the outback and whatever."

"Walkabouts in the outback." He scoffed. "Damn those *Crocodile Dundee* films."

"But I don't know what's going to happen to me when the game is over. I'm still trying to figure everything out."

"Eva." He sighed. "I meant it when I said you were different. You're the only one I want."

He deserved to hear me say that back to him. But I couldn't. I hung my head and twisted my hands together in my lap.

"What?" he asked. "What's really going on with you?"

I forced myself to meet his gaze and willed him to understand. "Since we met, I feel like the whole world is opening up to me. And now I see things . . . I have to follow my own path."

One corner of his mouth tugged up in a half smile. "So basically, it's my own fault you're dropping me flat?"

We ran out of things to say after that, but the silence between us was wistful, not angry. When we finally landed at LAX, Teague had a car waiting to drive us back to my apartment.

"I'll walk you to your door," he offered, handing me my overstuffed shopping bag.

"Don't you want to come in for a few minutes?"

"No, it's better if we leave it like this." He opened his door and circled the back of the car to open mine. "For now."

I managed a shaky smile. "'To be continued'?"

"Someday. Who knows?" We walked (really, really slowly) through the courtyard. "If you're ever in New York . . ."

"I'll call you. Promise." I stopped in front of my apartment. "And next time you're in L.A. . . ."

"I'll be knocking on this door."

I could feel his breath against my cheek. "I had a really nice weekend. You were the perfect person to take me on my first trip to Venice."

"And you were the perfect person to break my heart."
He kissed me softly.

"Stop." I kissed him back. "I didn't break your
heart."

"A little bit." He held his thumb and index finger
centimeters apart. "But that's just the kind of girl you
are. I told you so the first day I saw you."

I watched from the doorway as he walked back to the
car and out of my life.

# 21

The next morning, I woke up to the sounds of honking horns and the recycling collection crew emptying bins of glass and metal in the alley. No doubt about it, I was back in L.A. When I inhaled, I could practically taste the thick, brown smog.

"Eva?" Coelle called from the other side of my bedroom door. "You up yet?"

I squinted into the sunlight streaming in through the cheap vertical blinds. "I am now."

"I just signed for a package for you." Coelle kicked aside the clothes I'd discarded on the carpet yesterday, when I'd been too exhausted to care about wrinkles in my new outfits. She had laid off the heavy black eyeliner and microdresses and returned to her old standbys: yoga pants, Cornell T-shirt, and ponytail.

"You done being the devil?" I mumbled through my postflight cottonmouth.

"All except cashing the check. I filmed my last scene yesterday. Now Laurel's forcing me go out for a bunch of network pilots."

She sat down on the edge of my mattress, and I nudged her with my toe. "You're such a victim."

"Ain't it the truth? But my birthday's next week. I'll be eighteen and you know what that means—I get to start keeping my own money. My tuition fund is going to get bloated in a hurry."

I propped myself up on my elbows. "Hey, is Jacinda downstairs? I have to talk to her."

Coelle did a big, dramatic, Jacinda-y hair flip. "Please. She's got some new boyfriend and she spends every spare second with him."

I collapsed back into my pillow. "Urg."

"Don't worry—you know how she is with these guys. Although this one isn't her usual type—she says they go *running* together, if you can believe that."

I groaned. "The new boyfriend? It's my brother."

Coelle clapped her hands to her mouth. "No!"

"Yes."

She winced. "I'll pray for you—both of you."

"This isn't funny!"

"Well, here, maybe this will cheer you up." She rested a FedEx package on my stomach. "So where did Teague take you?"

I threw my arm over my eyes. "I don't want to talk about it."

"It didn't go well?"

"I don't want to talk about it," I repeated. I didn't want to share Venice with anyone but Teague. Telling someone else would spoil it somehow.

She flicked my arm. "Cran-kee. What's wrong with you anyway? You've been sleeping for fifteen hours."

"Jet lag."

She gasped. "From where? Eva, come on, where did you guys go? You have to tell me!"

"I don't have to do anything but pee and then sleep fifteen more hours."

"What a killjoy. Aren't you at least going to open your package?"

I opened my eyes and examined the shipping label on the box. The postmark was Italian. "Yeah, but you have to leave. This is private."

"Eva!"

"Just let me have five minutes alone! Sheesh! It's nothing personal. I just . . ."

"You were a lot more fun before you turned into a celebrity girlfriend." She flounced out and slammed the door.

"I'm not his girlfriend," I told the door. Then I grabbed a pair of scissors and ripped into the small cardboard box.

Inside, I found another box—a slim, hinged rectangle covered in black velvet. And when I opened that, I found . . .

"Oh my God." He'd sent me the sapphire-and-diamond earrings I'd coveted in that shop window by Piazza San Marco. The delicate jewels glittered like stars reflected in the Grand Canal. How had he known?

Then I found the white notecard tucked under the jewel box:

*For when you need to feel like royalty.*

No signature.

I held the earrings in the palm of my hand and let my skin warm the cool, glittery stones. Venice had changed me, that was for sure. I'd never be the same girl I was when I boarded the plane in LAX last Friday. I'd never be a virgin again, obviously, but it went deeper than that. Maybe some of Teague's confidence had rubbed off on me.

I reread the note and promised myself I'd never be afraid to go after what I wanted.

Then I picked up the phone and dialed.

"Hey." My voice sounded strong and steady. "Listen, I've been thinking . . . maybe we should try to work this out. Want to meet for coffee or something?"

# 22

The sun was shining and the palm trees were swaying in a gentle ocean breeze—another perfect SoCal afternoon. My newfound serenity had stayed with me through the day. I'd gotten ready for this date in five minutes flat: jeans, ballet flats, white T-shirt, and my new sapphire earrings. A little dressy, sure, but what was the point in having beautiful things if you just kept them locked up in a drawer because it wasn't a "special occasion"? Teague would surely approve. I reached up to touch my earlobes as I waited for the traffic light to change, then hurried across the street to the Coffee Beanery.

I spotted Danny immediately—the blue-and-yellow UCLA baseball cap was hard to miss. He'd staked out a table in the back corner and had placed a covered paper cup in front of the empty chair. A latte for me, hopefully.

"Hey." I couldn't help smiling when I approached the table.

He smiled, too. "Hey. I ordered for you, I hope you don't mind."

"Not at all. Thank you." I picked up the latte and sipped—yep, he'd gotten it exactly right.

"Okay." He braced himself like he was about to be drawn and quartered. "Go ahead. Get it all out."

I choked on my latte. "What?"

"I know what you're going to say. If we're going to work this out, you have to get closure on the breakup. I know."

I shook my head. The new Eva Cordes didn't fritter her life away on stuff like closure. "Let me ask you something: Do *you* want to talk about closure?"

"Hell, no," he said. And if I wasn't very much mistaken, he was not-so-subtly checking me out in my new jeans.

"Okay, then. Let's save closure for another day. Right now, let's just get down to basics. You said you missed me."

He looked me square in the eye and I felt something I'd never felt with Teague. "I do."

"And I miss you. But I'm tired of all the angst and the drama."

He leaned in. "Agreed. We should start over."

"Hmm. Interesting. Like we just met?"

"Total strangers on our first blind date."

"I like it." But the way we were looking at each other was not very blind date-y. It was more get-kicked-out-of-the-coffee-bar-for-excessive-PDA-y.

"All right, then." He got to his feet and pulled out my chair. "Would you like to sit down?"

I grinned. "Nope."

He blinked. "No? But—"

"You know what?" I leaned over and kissed him. Quickly, but very thoroughly. "I think we're good for today."

"Eva, wait!"

"Looking forward to our second date." I strutted toward the door and raised my hand in a jaunty backward wave. "Call me."

\* \* \*

"Pass the syrup," I mumbled through a mouthful of Belgian waffle the next morning. "And the butter. And the orange juice. And the napkins."

"Good Lord, girl, did Teague *starve* you over the weekend?" Coelle marveled, handing over the tall carafe of freshly squeezed orange juice. Through some freak-ish alignment of the stars, everyone—and I do mean *everyone*—had managed to get together for breakfast at the little café down the street from our apartment at the crack of dawn on Tuesday.

"Yeah, really." Jacinda stopped feeding my brother bites of her flax-laden oatmeal (I know!) long enough to narrow her eyes at me. "Something's different about you. Where did you guys go?"

"I'll never tell." I took another huge bite of waffle and whipped cream.

My mother beamed with pride. "I can't believe an A-list celebrity ran away with you for a lost weekend of passion. My baby's all grown up!"

"Mom!"

"Don't talk with your mouth full, darling." She turned to Thomas. "So are you ready for your big show this weekend?" We didn't know who she'd talked to or what she'd said, but my mom had managed to finangle a booking for Thomas's band at the hottest new club on the Strip. Evidently she still had some pull with her old rock 'n' roll connections.

Thomas started sweating visibly at the very mention of his Hollywood debut.

"You'll be great," Jacinda said, stroking his bicep.

"Stop, I'm trying to eat," Coelle groused. "And since when do you get up this early?"

"Don't hate just because I could run your ass into the ground any day of the week," Jacinda said sweetly.

"Oh please. You wish that were true."

"No, she's fast," Thomas said. "I can barely keep up with her."

Jacinda purred, "You keep up with me in all the ways that count."

"That's it, I'm throwing up," Coelle said.

I raised my hand. "Me, too."

"Girls." Aunt Laurel stopped sneaking strips of bacon down to Rhett in his Louis Vuitton carrier and gave us a stern look. "No pointless bickering until after nine A.M., please. I don't arbitrate off the clock."

"Fine. But just so you know, I'm a damn gazelle," Jacinda told her. "I'm thinking major Nike ad campaign. Maybe Adidas. Look into it."

Laurel whipped out her BlackBerry. "That's not a bad idea, actually."

"Wait and see." Jacinda looked around the table triumphantly. "I'm going to be the poster child for healthy living. Athletic, preppy, clean-cut . . ."

"Hey, speaking of which, whatever happened with Pemberley?" I asked. "Did you guys work it out?"

She and Thomas shared an exasperated, superior look. "I tried. I told her a hundred times what happened with Chip at the engagement party, but she just won't listen. She says she knows he's not perfect, but she loooves him . . ."

"I've been there." My mom sipped her dark roast coffee. (Supermodels don't eat breakfast. Or lunch. Or dinner.) "I *invented* 'but I love him.' She is in for a world of hurt." Her eyes lit up. "Hey, do you think she'd be willing to go on my show? I'm making the girls over, inside and out."

"I'll ask her." Jacinda didn't sound optimistic.

"It's okay." Thomas kissed her cheek. "She'll come around."

Thomas and Jacinda were so wrong together, they were almost . . . right. She seemed calmer and he seemed happier.

That was the tricky thing about love: You never ended up with the person who looked perfect on paper.

I stopped talking and laughing for a minute and

wondered what Teague was doing right now. Maybe I'd visit him in New York. Maybe not—maybe what we had shared was better left alone.

My aunt was watching me closely. "Nice earrings."

I touched the dangling sapphires. "Thanks."

She put her hand over mine. "You sure you don't want to talk about what happened last weekend?"

I shook my head. "But actually, I do have something else I need to talk to you about. The whole acting thing . . ."

"The director was very pleased with your work," she assured me. "He called me when filming wrapped. And *Westchester County* will look great on your résumé." She shot a venomous glare at Jacinda, but didn't mention the script-throwing meltdown.

"Well, that's the thing." I picked at my cuticle. "I'm not sure I want to act anymore."

Dead silence around the table. I didn't look up, but I could feel everyone staring at me.

"It's been . . ." oh so many adjectives to choose from ". . . interesting. But I don't think it's what I want to do with the rest of my life."

"But you're so good at it," Laurel said at the same time my mom said, "But you're so photogenic."

"Quit," Coelle advised.

Jacinda tsk-tsked. "I'm telling you, you've got to have the passion."

"I know." I sighed. "And I don't have the passion. I want to get back to my real life."

"This is your real life," my aunt pointed out.

She was right. This was my family, gathered around that table. We were odd and contentious and hopelessly dysfunctional, but we were family. When had that happened?

"Oh, darling, no." My mom looked hurt, but she didn't break out the usual hysterics. "You're moving back to Massachusetts? But we're just starting to—"

"No, no," I assured her. "I'm not taking my scholarship to Leighton. Besides the fact that everyone in my graduating class hates my guts, I'm pretty sure I couldn't take the cold anymore. There's a lot to be said for seventy-degree winters. I'm thinking of applying to UCLA."

Coelle's eyebrows shot up.

"And USC," I hastened to add. "Maybe Pomona, Claremont McKenna . . ."

"So you'll stay out here for the next four years, at least?" Mom asked.

"That's the plan."

"Oh, thank God." She collapsed with a whimper of relief on my aunt's shoulder. "My baby, my baby."

"Mari!" Laurel twisted away. "You're getting mucus on my suit!"

Some things never change.

"Excellent." Coelle rummaged through her huge leather tote and produced a folder emblazoned with a red *C*. "We can be application buddies. I've already started writing my essay for Cornell: 'Everything I Need to Know About Life I Learned From a Daytime Soap Opera.'"

"Oh, I almost forgot," Jacinda said. "I got that letter for you. It's sitting on the kitchen table." She paused. "Or in my bedroom. Somewhere in the apartment."

"That narrows it down," Coelle said.

"What letter?" I asked.

"Jacinda's dad is coercing one of the Cornell trustees to write me a letter of recommendation," Coelle explained.

"It was the least I could do to make up for my, uh, recent indiscretions." Jacinda cleared her throat.

Thomas turned to her. "What kind of indiscretions?"

"Nothing important," she said quickly. "Just girl stuff."

Coelle smirked at me. "UCLA, huh?"

"Maybe." I lifted my chin. "It's close by, and it's a great school."

"Uh-huh."

"What?" My mom motioned Coelle in. "What's the scoop with UCLA?"

"No scoop," I said firmly.

"Is it a boy?"

"Mom . . ."

"It is, isn't it?" She elbowed Laurel. "The Cordes legacy continues."

Jacinda lunged across the table. "You're back with Danny?"

"I have no comment," I said. "My client does not wish to discuss her personal life at this time."

"Good girl." Laurel looked proud. "Maybe you should go into PR."

Maybe I should. Maybe I would. I had no idea what the next four years would bring, and that was fine by me.

Right on cue, my phone rang and I pushed my chair back. "Excuse me, guys, I have to take this."

*"Oooooh,"* my roommates, my mother, and my aunt singsonged in unison.

"Let me guess," Thomas said. "UCLA?"

I made a face and escaped out to the sidewalk before flipping open the Filament. The roads were snarled with irritable commuters, but the early-morning sky was clear and streaked with pink. "You rang?"

"I rang." Danny's voice was low and teasing. "I met this amazing girl on a blind date and then she pulled a Cinderella."

"You don't say."

"Yeah, she kissed and ran."

"How rude."

"And I'm dying to see her again."

"Hmm, well, this girl . . . what does she like to do? Besides kiss, I mean?"

"Well, she has been known to hang out in nice restaurants with extensive dessert menus."

I twisted a lock of hair around my index finger. "Sounds very high-maintenance."

"So I was hoping she might meet me for dinner tonight at Dice? At, say, eight o'clock?"

"Eight o'clock," I mused. "She might be able to pencil you in."

"I know you're in demand. Places to go, people to see . . ."

"True." I laughed up at the rising California sun. "I'm a woman of the world, you know. Consider me on my way."